Revelation of a Storm

Written by

Inspire wise

This book was written with love and creativity given through life experiences that caused an evolution of a storm.

CONTENTS

CHAPTER 1

A Hurricane

Dahlia tightly held her three-year-old son Mecca's hand as they walked up the street to the neighborhood park. This time though, it wasn't a play date, but mentally beneficial for the both of them. Every so often they would go to the park at night and stare at the stars. For Mecca it was educational; for Dahlia, it was more therapeutic. She didn't know why, but for some reason, the stars had some sort of healing effect on her. So, whenever she was stressed or just needed to think, she would always look toward the heavens. The last couple of times, Mecca had been on a quest, to find this Big Dipper, formed by a group of stars that his mother had told him about.

Dahlia laid in the grass, staring at the stars. She closed her eyes, took a deep breath and sighed heavily as she

Inspire wise

released it. Her life was headed towards a major change, and she didn't know which direction she'd take. She tried to act like she had it all together, but she was lowkey scared. It was a different world than which she was used to living in, and now she had more than just herself to worry about.

Dahlia stared at Mecca as he laid down beside her, reminiscing being around his age. Those were happy times, when she was without a worry in the world. She remembered having one best friend, her grandfather Marcellus. Thinking about him was bittersweet because he had died nine years prior.

Dahlia and her grandpa were extremely close, with him playing a major role in her life. She remembered being a young girl, around four or five, and him and her sitting on the porch watching the stars light up the night sky.

"Boy, do I miss you," she mumbled to herself, as the tears built in her eyes.

"What's wrong mommy?" Mecca asked.

"Nothing sweetheart," Dahlia responded, trying to prevent a single tear from escaping. Dahlia certainly knew one thing for sure. If she didn't have anything else, she had him, and to her, that was all she needed.

Dahlia was only 18 when Mecca was born, and they'd been on their own for a couple of months now.

"Nothing pumpkin," she responded, kissing him on his forehead. "Wow, Mecca!! Do you see that? It's the Big Dipper!" She pointed towards the sky and pulled him closer towards her. She finally got his eyes to see the cluster of stars in the sky.

"I see it mommy!" Mecca yelled with excitement, as his eyes opened wide in amazement. *"This is what it's all about,"* Dahlia thought, *"— the memories."*

"Whoa!" they both said with excitement and in disbelief as they witnessed a star shoot across the sky. *"It can't get any better than this,"* Dahlia thought to herself. She always felt as though it was something magical going on up there, and she always wanted Mecca to experience it. *"Perfect timing."*

Dahlia looked at Mecca's innocent yet excited little face while he watched the sky with amazement. "You have to make a wish, Mecca."

They both stood in silence. She knew Mecca was making his wish and for the first time, Dahlia herself made a wish upon a star. They both continued surveilling the heavens, even long after the star had gone, hoping that it was holding something else magical. The universe now had them hypnotized and they couldn't look away, afraid they would miss something extraordinary.

After concluding that the show was now over, Dahlia felt it was time to leave. Besides, they had a busy day tomorrow. "Come on Mecca," she said. "Time to go home." Dahlia packed up their things, and they slowly walked home, enjoying the view of the sky the entire way back. Dahlia bathed Mecca and put him to bed. She then showered and jumped in bed, she didn't want to stay up too late, because she had work the next day.

***

Beep... Beep....Beep! Dahlia's hand slapped the alarm clock before she swiped the snooze button. *"Just ten more minutes,"* she mumbled to herself before closing her eyes again. To Dahlia, ten minutes only seemed like one before the alarm blared off again. Dahlia swiped the alarm one last time, vowing to get up, and letting out a big sigh, visualizing the day that lied ahead. *"Another day...another dollar,"* she mumbled, peeling herself off her mattress and out of bed. She began starting her day as usual, getting herself and Mecca ready. She got them both dressed, fed, then off they went towards the bus stop.

The year was 1992. Dahlia and Mecca were living in a ran down duplex, in Norfolk Virginia. It wasn't what most people would call the best of neighborhoods. In fact, her street was one of the main streets that drug dealers, addicts, and prostitutes hung out. She never had issues with anyone though, and the few people that she did know, seemed pretty cool so far. Besides, it was a roof over their heads for now, and that's what truly mattered.

Dahlia tightly held Mecca's hand as they walked to the bus stop, only turning around when hearing someone calling her name. From a distance, she could see her best friend Roro running towards her. Roro was also tightly holding her son Jeremiah's hand, as he ran as fast as his little legs allowed him to. He learned throughout the years that he had to run fast in order to keep up with his mommy, and she made sure that he had plenty of practice because that chick was never on time for anything.

"Oh good... I thought I was gonna have to leave yo ass!" Dahlia yelled, deciding to walk towards her, so they wouldn't have to run so far.

Dahlia was grateful to have Roro as a friend and sister. No, they didn't share the same parents, nor blood, but they've been inseparable since the 5th grade. Many times, they even experienced the same situations. For example, when Dahlia told Roro that she was pregnant,

Roro's response was..."Me too!" Not only that, they went to hair school together, became hair stylists together, and now for the past month, worked at the same salon. They also understood each other's struggles, with them being two 21-year-old, single black mothers, trying to survive with their 3-year-old sons. Once Roro finally reached Dahlia, they proceeded to walk to the bus stop with their baby boys.

"Bitch! Why didn't you answer your phone last night, I was bored as hell! That ain't like yo ass," Roro said, still slightly out of breath. "If I didn't know any better, I'd be under the impression that you were getting some." Dahlia played ignorant, as if she didn't understand what Roro was talking about.

"Getting some what?"

"Some dick!" Roro blurted out, waiting on another response. But this time Dahlia didn't respond. She instead answered the question with a look, never having to open her mouth.

As far as Dahlia was concerned, there was absolutely nothing to explain. The only man that came anywhere near her bed was Mecca. Neither Dahlia nor Roro were even having conversations with dudes, let alone sex. And neither could see that happening any time in the near future.

"Girl I'm sorry," Dahlia said, sitting on the bench, at the bus stop. "I couldn't sleep at all last night."

"I understand," Roro replied as she sat on the bench beside Dahlia. "It gets better...trust me." She sat Jeremiah down beside her and wrapped her arm around him.

"I know," Dahlia agreed.

Dahlia began reminiscing about when things were much better, times when she had a more financially fulfilled life. It wasn't a rundown duplex, but a condo in Virginia Beach, close to her parents. She didn't have to catch the bus because she owned a brand new Acura Legend that her boyfriend bought her last year for her birthday.

Though it had only been two months later, she now had nothing but Mecca to call her own.

"Finally!... Here comes that slow ass bus," Roro said as she stood up.

"Okay off we go," Dahlia said to Mecca as she picked him up.

They all boarded the bus. Their first stop was to drop the boys off at daycare. Once they were dropped off, Dahlia and Roro caught another bus and headed to work—the same schedule they had every work day.

Later that day, after a long day of work Dahlia was extremely tired. It seemed more draining than usual because it was more mental than physical.

"So, what are we eating for dinner tonight?" Dahlia asked Mecca, looking down at him with a smile. What a beautiful smile it was, which he got honestly from her. Dahlia was a beautiful woman, with her short blonde colored hair, pecan brown complexion, tall and slim frame, yet curvy. She was amazed at how many features of hers he inherited.

"Candy!" Mecca yelled as he sat up on the couch.

"Nooo!" Dahlia yelled as she got up and walked to the kitchen. "Come help me." She motioned her hand, waving him to follow her towards the kitchen.

"Okay," he agreed, knowing he had no other choice.

"How about something quick? Like noodles?" she asked.

"Again, Mommy?" Mecca whined. Dahlia looked at his face, watching as he pouted and poked his bottom lip out, wanting to cry.

"I know Mecca...just one more night," Dahlia pled, copying him by poking her bottom lip out.

"Stop copying me!" he yelled, turning that poked out lip into a smile. Dahlia smiled back at him, still imitating everything he did. What Little Mecca didn't understand was how it pained her knowing that noodles was the only dinner she could actually afford.

"I can't wait to build my clientele up," she thought to herself. After they ate their noodles, Mecca fell peacefully asleep while Dahlia sat up in her bed and cried herself to sleep.

The next day was much better for Dahlia; she had a little more pep in her step. The weekend was here, and it was projected to be lit. Dahlia and Roro never get time to go out, but Roro's mom Mrs. Pat, decided to give them both a well needed break for the night.

"You girls stay out of trouble," she said, looking directly at Roro. Roro was much different than Dahlia when it came to personality. While Dahlia was more humble and reserved, Roro was live and down for whatever, and she had absolutely no filter. Mrs. Pat knew this, so instead of talking to Roro, she looked at Dahlia and told her to keep Roro out of trouble.

"Okay Mom," Dahlia responded.

After hearing a twenty minute lecture, on the do's and don'ts, they were free to finally go to Picasso's in Mrs. Pat's car. When Dahlia and Roro pulled up to the club, they immediately became excited. Shit, it had been a long time coming, and they could tell that it was jumping by the amount of cars in the parking lot. It was so packed that all of the parking spaces were taken. They had to park across the street in the 7-11 parking lot, on Newtown Road.

"Man...I hope they don't tow my momma's car," Roro mumbled as they crossed the street over to the Picasso's parking lot.

"Girl it's gonna be fine," Dahlia assured, praying she was right. It had been so long since being out, she not only wanted this but needed it...more than anything. When they walked in the club, they could feel all eyes were on them.

"Can you feel that thick ass shit?" Roro asked, wanting confirmation on the energy in the room.

"Yeah, I feel it," Dahlia replied as they walked through the club, peeping out their surroundings.

"Okay, I see you bitch!" Roro said, as if whomever she was talking about could hear her. It was said only loud enough for Dahlia to hear though. Dahlia caught the hint, following Roro's eyes across the room and straight into the eyes of one of Roro's enemies. It was her...Jeremiah's father's new girlfriend.

The new girlfriend was with three other women, but none of that mattered to Roro. She didn't give a fuck how many people was with her. If anything popped off, she was always ready. She had to be that way, because women hated her, mainly over jealousy.

Roro was equally as beautiful as Dahlia, only shorter and a little thicker, with long hair. She was used to a lot of women not liking her, because of her looks. They always seemed to underestimate her, for that reason alone. The crazy thing about it is usually by the time they realized their mistake, the beat down had already happened. Everyone in Norfolk knew Roro, and they also knew that she was by no means anyone to play with.

Roro and Dahlia walked around, surveying the club for even more potential enemies. After they fully scoped out the club, they found a spot where they could sit comfortably and enjoy the rest of their night.

"No bad energy tonight," Dahlia said, looking at Roro with a smile. "This is our night, fuck them miserable ass bitches."

"You're right, fuck them hoes!" Roro replied and stood up. "What are you drinking?"

Roro was ready to enjoy her night. She knew misery loved company, and she wasn't in the mood to entertain no miserable ass bitches.

"White Russian, shawtie!" Dahlia answered with a smile.

"Bitch...you and that milky ass shit!"

Dahlia giggled at Roro's remark, "Whatever hoe!"

They both laughed then Roro grabbed her purse and walked to the bar to get their drinks. Dahlia sat at the table, watching the scenery, and feeling the music. It felt good to be out, enjoying the night. It didn't last long before her peace was interrupted by someone yelling.

"Bring your ass over here!"

"Come on, bitch!"

"Naw, don't hold that triple x hoe back!"

She noticed the yelling was coming from the direction of the bar. "Roro! Oh hell naw!" Dahlia blurted out, as she stood up, looking in the direction of the bar trying to see what the hell was going on. She had to make sure that Roro had zilch to do with any of the drama. As she approached, Dahlia saw two bouncers holding Roro back, while Jason's girlfriend and her friends were yelling, "Let that bitch go!"

Dahlia quickly ran towards Roro. She knew she had to try to calm Roro down, but she knew her friend and calming her down was almost impossible once she really became angry.

"So, you're gonna let them ruin your night?... Fuck them dirty ass bitches!" Dahlia yelled, trying to get Roro to listen. "Fuck them bitches; they don't exist."

The bouncers walked off with Roro, still trying to get her to calm down. Dahlia walked close behind because she knew that if Roro was already angry, there was no way that they were going to calm her down. If anything, they would only make her angrier as she continued to replay the current events in her mind.

"You know what?" Dahlia said, trying to think of whatever she could to calm Roro down. "Fuck this shit, let's go to Upscales."

By that time, Roro wasn't trying to hear none of that. "Naw, fuck that!" Roro yelled. "Imma keep my black ass right here!!"

Dahlia pled with Roro to let the shit go. "It's our only night out! You're gonna let them ruin it! Remember our energy! We're not going to let low energy motherfuckers fuck up our vibes!"

But it was too late. Roro was angry as hell, and no one could calm her down, not even Dahlia. That's when the bouncers decided it was best for them to leave, so they escorted them both out. On their way out the club, Dahlia looked at the table where Jason's girl was sitting and noticed that all four of the women were gone. *"Not today,"* she told herself as she gently pushed Roro towards the exit.

Dahlia and Roro walked towards the car, only to walk right into Jason.

"So, you're in the club starting shit with my girl?" Jason asked Roro.

"Naw, yo bitch was fucking with me!" Roro said. Before she could begin to explain what happened, Jason punched her in her face, hard, like she was a man on the streets. As Roro fell to the grown, Dahlia jumped on his back, punching him everywhere her fist wanted to land with all her might. He never got the chance to react to Dahlia on his back, because some of the bouncers from the club had already started to beat him.

17

After the shock of her son's father hitting her, even more anger set in. Roro got up off the ground and she joined the bouncers by kicking and stomping Jason.

"Bitch," she yelled at him. "You hit me behind another bitch? I'll kill your ass!"

After some of the other bouncers grabbed her off and away from Jason, she put her focus back on the main issue. "Where are those bitches at?" she asked Dahlia.

"Where are you, you stupid ass bitches!" Roro yelled towards the crowd in the parking lot. "Don't hide now!" She yelled into the crowd. But to no avail, they were nowhere in sight. Dahlia finally convinced Roro to leave, explaining that the women were more than likely long gone.

After they left the club and were almost home, Roro had calmed down considerably. Dahlia explained to Roro how Jason's girlfriend had won, without them having to come to blows.

"That bitch created some drama, that wound up ruining your night. She had that all planned out once she seen you entering the club. Right now, I bet you anything, them bitches are somewhere making a fucking toast, for being able to control your peace of mind."

"Yeah, your right," Roro agreed. "Imma see them bitches again though. Trust me this shit ain't over. And next time when I do, I'm fucking them up, on sight. If I see any of them bum ass bitches again, I'm going straight to jail."

Dahlia wondered if Roro heard anything that she had just said. She knew in her heart that Roro was serious, and it was only a matter of time before Roro would see her ex's new girlfriend again.

Dahlia laid in her bed that night, thinking about everything that happened at the club. *"Why would he put his hands on her like that? And what did he expect me to do, just stand there?"* Dahlia wondered. *"Him, out of all the people in the world, know that she's partially crazy."* She kept replaying the night and closed her eyes.

"Leave me alone!" Dahlia yelled.

She ran down a dark street, that she has never been down, and doesn't understand how she got there. There was a tall medium built guy running fast behind her. The faster she ran, the slower she moved. Just when he reached out to grab her, she woke up.

Beep... Beep... Beep! Dahlia opened her eyes. *"What the fuck was that dream about?"* Dahlia asked, looking at the alarm clock. *"Damn it's only 3:00?"* she mumbled with regret because now she was wide awake and couldn't go back to sleep. She sat up in the bed and opened her blinds to look at the stars.

"Grandad!" she called out, sighing right afterward. "I miss you so much!"

Thinking of him always took her down memory lane. She remembered as a child, having nightmares and waking up in the middle of the night scared. Every one of those nights, he was always prepared, like he knew which days to stay up, and which to go to sleep. He was always there for her, especially on those nights, he would always be up waiting.

Her grandfather was her hero, in the flesh. Even his voice was heroic to her. She remembered how his voice sounded when he sung to her. His voice was very deep, but met with a soft tone. It was the perfect voice to soothe her sleepless nights. So many memories, she thought...so much love.

Beep beep beep! *"Damn it's that time again already?"* she thought as she swiped the alarm clock. *"Another day,"* she sighed. She got out of bed and began to get her and Mecca dressed for the day that lie ahead. She followed her daily routine, but the buses ran a little late.

Dahlia ran to the door of her job, after arriving at least 15 minutes late. By the time she put her bag in the station, she heard the receptionist yell across the room, "Dahlia you have a request!"

"Okay," Dahlia yelled back, setting up her station as fast as she could.

Once she got everything situated, Dahlia looked up to see which one of her clients were waiting. She was happy to see it was one of her favorite clients, Jane. Jane had been getting her haircut by Dahlia since hair school and followed her to this salon.

"Hey lady!" Dahlia said, happy to speak to her client.

Jane opened her arms, greeting Dahlia with a big hug. "Hey my favorite stylist."

The feeling that Jane had for Dahlia was mutual. She just prayed that Dahlia wouldn't stop doing hair. She was tired of trying to follow stylist, but the way she felt about Dahlia, she would have to go to her house— that's it, case closed.

Dahlia and Jane proceeded to walk to Dahlia's station.

"So, what's been going on?" Dahlia asked, letting the black styling cape flow with the wind before fastening it around Jane's neck.

"Nothing much," Jane replied, enjoying the feeling of being pampered after a long week of work. "When are you gonna buy one of these houses?" She held her head down, so Dahlia could comb through her long grey hair.

"I don't know," Dahlia responded, holding Jane's head, so that it wouldn't move.

Jane was a successful real estate agent. Her and Dahlia had become very close over the years and every time she seen Dahlia, she talked to her about buying a house. She didn't have to buy it from her, even though she would give her a better deal than anyone else. She knew that it would be a life changing experience for both Dahlia and Mecca.

Dahlia would have loved to own a house, but she knew that she couldn't afford it at this time. Jane watched Dahlia's facial expression and could almost feel her thoughts.

"You know it's not as hard as you think," she reassured Dahlia.

"I know, I'll let you know when I'm ready," Dahlia said before quickly changing the subject. "So, what's been going on with you?"

Dahlia listened to all the new things going on in Jane's life, and at the same time daydreamed of her and Mecca one day opening the door of their beautiful two story house, with a two door garage. Just the thought of it felt good. Although Jane always talked to Dahlia about buying a house, for some reason, this time felt different.

When Jane first asked Dahlia about buying a house, Dahlia was still in a relationship with her son's father Smoke, and during that time, Smoke didn't want to buy a house. "It's only us three," he would say..."We don't need that much damn room." If only she knew then why he was really saying that, it probably would have saved her a lot of heartache. She later found out that he wanted to buy a house, he just didn't want to buy one with her.

Now that it was just her and Mecca, she wanted something more stable and secure for her and her three-year-old son. But it seemed as if now the dream was more out of reach. *"Life has to be better than this,"* she thought to herself as she softly combed Jane's hair before trimming her ends.

"Girl it was busy today," Roro said with a big grin on her face as she found a seat on the bus. She scooted close to the window to make enough room for Dahlia to sit beside her.

"Yeah, you were busy bitch, as usual, not me," Dahlia said lapping her eyes.

"Girl, give it time."

Roro had been doing hair since they were twelve. By the time she was sixteen, the whole neighborhood was coming to her to get the latest hairstyles. Braids, weave, wigs, haircuts, whatever—she enjoyed doing it all.

Dahlia on the other hand, only did it because of Roro. It was just a job to her, and she could still be with her best friend while at work. *"Shit, we do everything else together anyway, why not hair,"* Dahlia thought. Besides, she didn't have a clue about what she really wanted to do.

Smoke had taken care of Dahlia financially from the time she became pregnant with Mecca. She hadn't had the chance to do anything on her own yet. She always thought that him, her, and Mecca would always be together. She was just now trying to find her place in the world. At this point, she was doing anything that would support her and Mecca, just until she could sort it all out. So, hair it was.

Dahlia was playing with Mecca when she heard the phone ring. She reached over to look at the caller I.D. to see who was calling. "*Hmmm,*" she wondered. "*I never seen this number before.*"

Only a handful of people knew her number, which made her contemplate whether or not to even answer the phone call. Eventually hearing the phone ring on and on, got the best of her curiosity. "Let me answer this damn phone, it might be about something important," she thought, finally deciding to pick it up.

"Hello," she answered.

"Hello," the familiar voice replied.

Once Dahlia figured out who was on the other end, she felt a deep knot in the pit of her stomach.

"How are you?" he asked.

"How did he get this number?" she asked herself. "What do you want Smoke?" And how did you get my number?"

"I have my ways," he responded. "So, I hear that you moved to Reservoir." Letting her know, without outwardly saying to her, that wherever she went, he'd follow.

Dahlia was shocked that he got her number, and even more that he already knew where she lived. She was speechless. She didn't even know if she should respond to his question or not. She didn't feel like it was any of his business where her and Mecca lived. All he needed to know was that Mecca was well taken care of, with the help of her parents.

"Damn, I can't move no fucking where in Virginia, without him finding me," she thought. *"And how in the hell did this nigga get my number?"* Dahlia didn't do much talking. She opted to stay quiet, so she could hear the reason behind the phone call. It's been two months since she heard from him, and the pain was still fresh.

"So, you took my son, just to move to the hood, of all places," he said, downing her and the area she lived in. "Where is my son?"

Dahlia didn't like the fact that after everything that happened, the only thing that he could come up with, after being away from his son for two months, was to take a dig at where she was living.

"He's in his room, inside of our cozy little home in the ghetto. I have to go," she said and hung up the phone.

She ignored all other calls that night. *"Why did he even call me. This is the first time I've heard from him in months, why the sudden change now?"* she wondered. Dahlia felt as though Smoke wanted her to suffer. It seemed like he got a thrill from seeing her hurting. She continued to think about it, feeling her eyes become heavier and she slowly drifted off to sleep.

Dahlia tried to open the front door as fast as she could. She looked behind her and seen the same tall, medium built man running down the stairs behind her. He was trying to stop her from opening it. For some reason,

Dahlia couldn't turn the door knob. The man was gaining traction, with Dahlia desperately trying to open it.

"This is it," she told herself. She felt as though she had no choice but fight her assailant. Once he got close enough, Dahlia tried to get a better glimpse of his face. The only thing she could see was the shadow of his beard. The hoodie fell perfectly over his face, making it harder to see. Only a small highlight was visible from the moon as he reached out his arms to grab her.

Beep, beep, beep! Dahlia, once again, was saved by the alarm clock. Dahlia was more than happy to hear the alarm that morning. This was the second dream about this lunatic. *"Who could he be?"* she thought, knowing she don't fuck with nobody. Dahlia laid in the bed a bit longer, trying to figure out who fit what little description of him that she did have. Better yet, why in the hell was the brotha so angry.

Before she knew it, a half an hour went by, and she was running late for work. She rushed to get her and Mecca dressed and ran out the front door. She became angry with the door because she had to fight to lock it. While she held Mecca's hand as tight as she could, she ran up the street.

"Oh no!" she yelled, noticing that Roro and Jeremiah were nowhere in sight.

Roro was always late for everything, but Dahlia was extra late and Roro still wasn't there. She knew, for the first time, she was later than her friend and had missed her bus. *"Damn...now I know how Roro feels,"* she said as she turned around and walked back toward the house. She looked to the left before crossing the street and immediately got that knotted up, gut feeling again. She watched her old car driving towards her. Smoke happily grinned, noticing that Dahlia had missed her bus.

"Do you need a ride," he asked.

"No thank you," she quickly responded, holding Mecca's hand even tighter.

"Daddy!" Mecca yelled after hearing his father's voice.

This assumingly touched Smokes heart, so he pulled into the 7-11 parking lot. Dahlia's intention was to keep walking, but she also understood that Mecca wanted to see his father. She decided to wait to allow Smoke to talk to his son. She didn't want to be the one to rain on Mecca's parade, because his father already did that so well.

"Hey lil man," Smoke said approaching Mecca with his arms stretched out. Mecca ran into his father's arms as Smoke picked Mecca up, and hugged him, the whole time looking at Dahlia. He kissed Mecca on the cheek and walked towards the car. "Imma take y'all home."

Dahlia knew Smoke was using Mecca to get whatever it was that he wanted. What could she do though, she felt stuck between a rock and a hard place. She sighed as she followed behind Smoke and Mecca towards her car. They got into the car, and he drove them home.

Smoke parked in front of Dahlia's duplex.

"What's up," he asked, glancing at Mecca sitting in the backseat.

"Nothing's up," Dahlia responded, looking out the passenger window. She looked underneath the bushes, annoyed with the trash littered underneath.

"You understand that I didn't mean for things to play out the way they did right," Smoke began to explain.

"I remember everything that you told me," Dahlia said, opening the car door. She wasn't in the mood to reminisce on anything that happened between them. And most definitely, not in front of Mecca.

"I have to call my job," she said, opening the car door.

"I'll take you to work," he said, hoping that she would agree. Instead , she told him, "No thank you", and got out of the car. He already knew her phone number and where she lived. He would have to put in the same amount of energy to find out where she worked, because she wasn't telling that nigga shit!

As Dahlia got Mecca out of the car, Smoke told his son how much he loved him, and how he would stay in touch.

"I love you too, Daddy," Mecca replied, repping the same smile that his mother has. Dahlia powerwalked in the house, pulling Mecca close behind her, not looking back. *"That's the fakest love I've ever seen,"* she thought as she unlocked her door.

After Mecca went to bed, Dahlia was able to think more clearly, and without interruption. She loved Mecca with a passion, but she focused better when he slept. She tried her best to make sure that he didn't see any of the bad things that she was going through. Even when her and Smoke were going through their problems, she didn't want Mecca to know.

Dahlia thought back to before there was a Smoke. When there once was a man that loved her...her father did, unconditionally. She wished that she could witness his smile once more.

What Dahlia couldn't picture at the time, due to her being the young age she was, was that he would not always be there. She took that love for granted, and she wanted it back. She would do just about anything to see him again. In her mind, that was all she needed. *"Let me carry my ass to sleep,"* she thought to herself. *"Me and Roro got a lot of shit to do tomorrow."*

The next day after Dahlia and Mecca got dressed, they walked to Roro's house. Mrs. Pat was going to watch the boys, while Dahlia and Roro handled their affairs.

"Damn this line is long," Dahlia says as they walked toward the local human services building.

"You ain't never lied," Roro replied, irritated that she had to wait at the end of it. The line didn't bother Dahlia too much. Whenever her and Roro were in situations like this, they always made the best out of it. They would talk and laugh about silly shit. Anything to make the time go by.

After they stood in line for a while, they were finally near the front doors. As they continued to talk amongst themselves, they could hear someone at the back of the line laughing and talking loud. Once they turned around to see where all the unnecessary noise was coming from, they both were surprised. It was Roro's ex, Jeremiah's father Jason's, new girlfriend. The same bitch that was at the club that night. When his girlfriend finally noticed Roro and Dahlia looking at her, she smiled and continued to talk even louder to the girl standing beside her. All the while, never taking her eyes off Roro.

She made sure that they heard her this time. "I hate when Bitches stare at me. Say what the fuck you gotta say bitch, and let's get it over with."

Still, she stared at Roro not saying a word. The women were caught off guard as they watched the way her and Roro stared at each other. Being that they weren't at the club that night, they were totally in the dark.

Roro, on the other hand, was still fuming with anger over what happened at the club, now even angrier as she watched the girl staring at her, talking big shit. This girl wanted to push Roro's buttons, to get a reaction. So, to no avail, Roro gave her what she wanted.

"Bitch, what are you looking at!" Roro yelled, loud enough for her to hear at the end of the line, and anyone in between or close by for that matter.

Jason's girlfriend couldn't let Roro slide with a slick one out her mouth. "Fuck you... I'm looking at you bitch!" she yelled back at Roro.

They started walking towards one another yelling, telling each other what they were going to do to each other. As soon as Roro was in arms reach, she punched Jason's girlfriend in the face— all hell broke loose.

Dahlia and the girls that were with Jason's girlfriend, mutually decided to let them have a fair fight. Dahlia felt that as long as that bitch didn't get the best of Roro, and no one else jumped in, she was fine with it. Dahlia also knew that wasn't gonna happen. Just as she expected, Roro began to pounce away on her victim, forcing the new girlfriend to try everything in her power to fend off her attacker, but there was nothing she could do. Roro unleashed her anger on her from childhood and beyond.

By the time security pulled Roro off the girl, the new girlfriend was knotted up and glazed.

"I told you I was gonna see yo punk ass again, didn't I?" Roro yelled at her.

"Daaauuum!" You could hear some people in the crowd yelling, while others looked at Roro as if she were a wild animal or something, needing to be tamed. Dahlia followed behind Roro for the second time in a week, being escorted by security. This time though, Roro would be leaving with a court date.

"What happened?" Mrs. Pat asked Roro as soon as they entered the house.

"Ma," Roro began to explain, starting off with her usual. "Ma, it wasn't my fault." Mrs. Pat was almost immune to those words coming from Roro. Roro was always in trouble, ever since her and Dahlia were fourteen. She's spent months in juvenile detention, been on house arrest, fought the police, even got sarcastic with the judge. She's done a lot in her twenty-one years of life, so by now, you'd think she would come up with a better approach. And by the look on Mrs. Pat's face, she wasn't having it, those tactics had gotten old.

Mrs. Pat didn't comment on anything that Roro said, instead she looked at Dahlia. Dahlia held her head down, avoiding the urge to look up. "What happened Dahlia?" Mrs. Pat asked her. That was Dahlia's reason for holding her head down. She knew that Mrs. Pat was going to ask her what happened, and Dahlia hated lying to her.

Dahlia could feel Roro's eyes beaming at her, even without her looking in Roro's direction. She could also feel Roro telling her energetically, "You better not say shit." Even though Dahlia didn't hear those words come from Roro's mouth. *"Damn Roro,"* she thought, *"you put me on the spot again."*

Dahlia looked up at Mrs. Pat and explained, with the same old line as usual. She wouldn't totally lie to Mrs. Pat. Mrs. Pat knew that Dahlia always covered for Roro. She also knew that Dahlia, tried her hardest not to lie, so there were always more truths to her story then not. Usually, Mrs. Pat could sort through all of Dahlia's twist, and find out what really happened on her own.

"Ma," Dahlia began, trying to start off on Mrs. Pat's good side.

Dahlia started by telling Mrs. Pat the truth, beginning with them standing in line and hearing the women talking and laughing extremely loud behind them. She did, however, switch Roro and the other girl's roles around a few times, but only little things, like who said something first, or who threw the first punch. She also never mentioned that it was Jason's girlfriend that Roro was fighting. She kept that a secret because Mrs. Pat didn't ask. Dahlia considered them small lies, or white lies. She really tried to be honest with her second mother, yet and still, she didn't want to put her girl in more shit than she was already in. She already had to go to court— as far as Dahlia was concerned, she had learned her lesson. She didn't want Mrs. Pat angry at Roro, and she also knew that if Mrs. Pat felt like Roro was in any type of drama while having her car, it would be a cold day in hell before Mrs. Pat would ever let Roro drive her car again. So, for now, Dahlia and Roro were good.

After Roro and Dahlia finished listening to Mrs. Pat lecture Roro, on picking her battles and controlling her temper, they went to Roro's room.

"Man…if my momma had of restricted me from the car, I would've whipped that bitch's ass again!" Roro announced, hitting her hand with her fist.

"Bitch Mrs. Pat is going to whip your ass, keep it up," Dahlia joked, talking as low as possible, so Mrs. Pat wouldn't hear. Dahlia pictured Mrs. Pat running behind Roro's grown ass with a little switch. "Bitch, Mrs. Pat is gonna whip your ass!"

"Imma kill that bitch…it ain't over," Roro said, still thinking about what happened at the club that night and with Social Services. Beating the girls ass once, wasn't going to cut it for Roro.

Dahlia now looked at Roro with empathy. "There is no hope for you huh?"

"I do have hope though," Roro answered. "I do hope that I see that bitch walking in a dark alleyway with no witnesses."

"Okay bitch," Dahlia said, shaking her head. "If that bitch call the police on your ass, then what?" Roro looked at Dahlia with a straight...'dead men can't talk' look. "Bitch you need help, to conquer your kind of crazy."

"Yeah, I know," Roro replied, "but I'm a good kind of crazy though."

Dahlia couldn't understand why Roro could even begin to think that her crazy was "a good kind of crazy". She had to know.

"Well damn bitch," she asked. "What in the hell is a "good kind of crazy?"

Roro was confused herself about her comment. "How in the fuck would I know," she said. "The shit just sounds good, so whatever you consider crazy, that's me, how about that." Dahlia laughed.

Roro kept Dahlia laughing, mainly because Roro never thought before she talked. Instead, she had a habit of blurting out whatever came to her mind. And usually, after Dahlia would get her to think about whatever dumb shit she said, she would still try to justify herself. That, to Dahlia, was the funniest part of it all.

"Real shit though," Roro said. "How did momma know about what happened so damn fast?"

Dahlia was so caught up in explaining what happened, that she never thought about it. It was odd the way Mrs. Pat was onto them as soon as they opened the door. "Huh...that's a good question."

CHAPTER 2

Tropical Disturbance

O h no! I slept through the fucking alarm!" Dahlia yelled out once she opened her eyes and saw daylight shining through her mini blinds. "Oh shit!" She jumped out of bed, placing her feet on the floor. From out of nowhere, Dahlia burst into laughter. She realized she hadn't slept through the alarm after all. She smiled to herself, remembering she had cut it off because she had the day off. Another reason to smile was that Mecca was with his father. Since Smoke reconnected with his son, they've been inseparable. Dahlia crawled back in her bed, deciding to take advantage of the chance to be lazy for a change. *"What's wrong with laying here for a few more hours?"* she thought. Absolutely nothing because for the first time in months, she only had herself to worry about, and absolutely nothing to do.

Dahlia eventually got up, got herself dressed, fixed some breakfast, and headed over to Roro's house "by herself." She felt so free, and with her now well rested body, it felt so good.

"Yo, what's up?" Dahlia heard some guy speaking to her with an unfamiliar voice and accent as she walked towards Roro's house. She turned around to see who the man was. She looked up and locked eyes with the stranger. After getting a better look at him, his gaze was almost hypnotic. He was light complexioned, with not one mark on his face. He had red hair and was average height. She wondered if he worked out or if he was naturally built this way, his body was on point. *"Damn he fine!"* she thought again, looking back up at his face, and into the guy's peanut butter brown eyes.

"Damn he fine!" No matter what, her thoughts kept circling back to the beautiful distraction. She changed her mind about continuing to walk, opting to pause for a minute to hear him out instead. He was well-groomed,

leaning on a grey 1993 Max with tinted windows and 20 inch rims.

"What's up with you?" she finally responded smiling.

"Whatever. What's your name?" he asked.

"Why? I don't know you," Dahlia replied flirtatiously. "I don't give my name to strangers."

"That's what I'm saying!" the guy responded. "I don't want us to be strangers. By the way, my name is Rodney."

Dahlia looked at Rodney as he talked and couldn't deny how his gold teeth complimented his complexion. She didn't know exactly how many he had, but from what she seen, it was at least three. When Dahlia finally gave the guy her name, he repeated it. "Dahlia," he said, trying to keep it locked in his mind. Dahlia loved the way he sounded calling her name with his thick Jamaican accent.

"So, now that we're no longer strangers, you can talk to me, right?" he asked.

"I don't see a reason why not," Dahlia said. They talked for little while longer, exchanged numbers, and she continued her short journey to Roro's house, feeling even better about her day.

After leaving Roro's house later that night, Dahlia came home to an empty house. She took a shower, alone, ate a hamburger and fries, alone, and put a horror movie in the VCR to watch, alone. She missed Mecca but enjoyed her time, alone. *"I wonder how long Smoke is gonna keep him,"* she thought, trying to focus her mind back on the movie she was watching.

"I hate Smoke," she mumbled, immediately remembering the reason behind their breakup. Those hurtful memories would still come to her from time to time, and when they did, they always popped out of nowhere. This time, it was too hard to get her focus back. Dahlia replayed bits and pieces of the breakup in her mind as she closed her eyes.

"Fuck you!" she remembered him yelling at her. "Get the fuck out and fuck you!" Out of everything he said to her that night, those words stuck out the most. She knew the reason why he said it, and that reason alone was painful. While Dahlia was in deep thought, the phone rang, causing Dahlia to look at the caller I.D..

"Hey ma," she said after putting the phone against her ear.

"Hey baby," her mother replied. "Are you and Mecca okay?"

"Yeah, we're fine," Dahlia assured her mom. "How are you and dad?"

"We're doing pretty good, we just wanted to check on you and Mecca. Where is my baby by the way?"

"He's with Smoke," Dahlia said.

"Smoke!" Dahlia's mother yelled. "Wait, what? How in the hell did that happen?"

Dahlia explained to her mom the turn of events that led to Mecca being with his father and to her and Smoke finally being on speaking terms.

Mrs. Dot, Dahlia's mother, is a petite feisty woman, with a lot of bark to go along with her bite. Dahlia knew that she had to explain the situation clearly to let her know that things were okay.

"Okay now," Mrs. Dot said. "You've been making excuses and covering for Smoke for years...no matter what he do. You're gonna get tired of that shit one day. Hopefully nothing too crazy would have to happen." Mrs. Dot never involved herself with Dahlia and Smoke's relationship, but when it came to Mecca, shit could get real heavy. That went for anyone, including Dahlia.

Once Dahlia explained it more, Mrs. Dot was sure everything was fine. She asked Dahlia if she needed anything.

"No mom, I'm fine," Dahlia said, the same thing she always said. Dahlia never wanted to stress her parents out with too much. She would get a little help every now and then, only if she really needed it. But she didn't want to seem helpless. Besides, it would make them right about trying to get her and Mecca to move back home with them.

Dahlia wanted to be independent for once in her life. So what if she lived in the ghetto or used public transportation to get around. She was doing things by herself for the first time and without anyone's help. She couldn't let anyone see her fail. Dahlia and Mrs. Dot talked for a couple of hours on the phone and eventually hung up. Dahlia watched the movie until she fell asleep.

The next morning Dahlia sat at the bus stop waiting on Roro. *"This girl is always running late,"* she thought, looking up the boulevard for the bus, then back down the lane, hoping to see Roro with Jeremiah running helplessly behind her. The bus arrived and Roro was still nowhere in sight, forcing Dahlia to board the bus without her.

When Dahlia got off work that day, she decided to stop by Roro's house to find out why she didn't make it to work. When she walked up to the house, she noticed that Mrs. Pat's car was gone. *"Maybe she's not feeling well,"*

Dahlia thought as she knocked on the door. *"Weird."* Her knocks went unanswered. *"I'll call her later,"* she mumbled as she walked away.

When walking home, Dahlia could sense that she was being watched. She looked up, right before walking past a group of guys with all eyes are on her. She's used to the attention, so she never paid it any mind. But once she reached them, she noticed that not one guy said anything. *"This is odd,"* she thought to herself. *"This never happens to me."*

"Hey yo!" someone yelled. Dahlia turned around and saw Rodney, the guy she had met yesterday, jogging towards her. She stopped walking, and waited for him to catch up. "What's up?" he asked, showing off his handsome smile.

"Nothing much," Dahlia responded in what she hoped was the sexiest voice that she could.

"Did you lose my number?" he asked sarcastically.

"Did you forget mine?" she responded, equally as sarcastic as he was.

"Of course, I didn't. What are you getting ready to do?" Before she could start her sentence, he joined in and finished it for her, "I know, you don't know me!" Dahlia smiled, which in return made him smile harder. "Well, how about you get to know me? Are you cool with that?" he asked.

"Yeah, I'm cool with that."

Rodney walked Dahlia home but didn't leave. They sat on Dahlia's porch talking for hours. *"He seems pretty cool,"* Dahlia thought, listening to him describe what it was like growing up in New York and in Jamaica.

"Oh, how old were you when you lived in New York?" Dahlia interrupted. He explained how as a young boy he got in so much trouble that his parents felt they didn't have any other choice but to move to America. He began describing the differences between living in New York and living in Jamaica. As he spoke, Dahlia watched him closer. Something about him was intensely intoxicating.

He was exotic mixed with handsome. A beautiful combination.

"Yoooo!" one of Rodney's friends yelled to him from the crowd of guys up the street.

"Look, I gotta go. Imma call you, okay?" he assured.

"Okay," Dahlia said as she stood up to walk in the house.

"I would hug you, but I don't want to be rejected," Rodney said, trying to make the most pitiful face he could.

"Nah, no hugs tonight," she said and they both giggled.

"Okay, hopefully tomorrow," he replied, indicating that he was coming over tomorrow.

"Maybe," Dahlia responded smiling as she walked toward the door. He waited for her to close the door, then left.

"So, what's on tv?" she asked herself . All of a sudden, she heard her front door open and close. She looked up to see a guy she had never seen before walking toward her.

"I'm sorry," he said trying not to scare her. "But the police is chasing me." Dahlia didn't know what to do. She was home by herself, thank GOD because she really didn't know what she would have done if Mecca was there.

"I understand, but you can't stay here," Dahlia told the young man. "You have to leave."

"I'm not going anywhere," he responded as if he already knew her response.

Dahlia had to think quick. She didn't know him, therefore she didn't know what he was capable of doing, so making him mad was out of the question. All of a sudden, a memory of something similar that happened with Smoke came to her. She remembered one time when Smoke had been running from the police and a stranger came out of nowhere and gave him a hat and coat.

Dahlia went in her closet and grabbed an old hoodie that used to be Smoke's, but somehow wound up hers.

"Here is something that you could put on, but you have to go."

The young man took the hoodie. "I'm not leaving until they do," he said. And from the sound of his voice, that was exactly what he meant. Dahlia didn't know what to do. There she was, standing in her living room, face to face with a strange man that she never invited in.

The guy constantly went back and forth to the window, checking to see if the police had left. About 30 minutes later, the young man thanked Dahlia for letting him stay there.

"I don't see them anymore," he said. He then put on the hoodie Dahlia gave him and walked toward the door.

"You're welcome, but you didn't give me any other choice," she responded sarcastically, locking the door as she closed it behind him.

This was for sure a different type of neighborhood than she was used to. The days of leaving her door unlocked were in the past. *"That will never happen again,"* she mumbled. It was hard for Dahlia to fall asleep that night. She kept thinking about how things could have turned out much worse than they did, and how if it had, it would've been due to her own negligence. She couldn't afford to make mistakes like that, especially not now...being the protector of a 3 year old boy. Dahlia finally nodded off to sleep.

Beep beep beep! "Damn already!" Dahlia yelled as she cut off the alarm clock. *"It's another day,"* she mumbled, dragging herself out of bed.

Dahlia jumped in the shower, got dressed and off to the bus stop she went. Like any and all the other days, Dahlia waited for Roro. *"What the fuck is going on?"* she thought, staring down the empty street. *"This shit don't feel right."* Against her gut feeling, she slowly boarded the bus and continued with her regular schedule.

When Dahlia finally got off of work, she decided to walk to Roro's house. *"Good, Mrs. Pat's car is here,"* she thought as she walked to the door. She knocked twice and walked in, just like she always did.

Dahlia was the only person who could do that besides family, and to Mrs. Pat she was just that. She had known Dahlia since she was a child and she loved her as if she were her own. No one else in the neighborhood dared to do so. For one, no one wanted any smoke from Roro nor her family. And two, Mrs. Pat was a spiritual woman that the neighborhood respected as a whole. If someone were to do something crazy, they would have to constantly look over their shoulders.

"Hey, Ma," Dahlia yelled as she entered the house.

"Hey baby," Mrs. Pat yelled back. Dahlia followed her voice to the kitchen.

"Where is your crazy daughter?" She saw Mrs. Pat busy frying chicken.

"In jail," Mrs. Pat replied as if trying to hold back tears.

"What happened?" Dahlia asked, also trying to hold back her tears to be strong for Mrs. Pat.

Mrs. Pat began to explain the charges to Dahlia. Jason's new girlfriend had lied and said that Roro beat her with some kind of weapon.

"What!" Dahlia yelled. "That's not true Mrs. Pat, I was right there!"

Mrs. Pat looked at Roro, "I know that sweetheart and I wasn't even there, but that's what that devil is telling them people. Roro has a bond hearing tomorrow and more than likely she'll get out."

"Can I ride with you?" Dahlia blurted out before Mrs. Pat could finish talking.

"No, you can't...You have work tomorrow! You have to take care of little Mecca."

Dahlia already had a plan. "I can call out. It's rare that I do that, so they wouldn't mind."

Dahlia went on trying to explain different reasons why Mrs. Pat should let her go. Some, if not all, of the reasons were very convincing, but Mrs.Pat still wouldn't hear it. She knew, and had seen with her own eyes, how Dahlia and Roro struggled. There was no way that she was going to allow Dahlia to miss a day from work. Once Dahlia realized that she was unable to convince Mrs. Pat, she gave her a tight hug before walking home.

Once Dahlia made it back to her home, she couldn't help but still worry about Roro. She heated up the to-go plate Mrs. Pat was sure to slip her before she left. She sat at the kitchen table eating the chicken when the phone rang. She got up from the table and answered it.

"Hello," Dahlia answered, still chewing.

"Come outside," Rodney's voice rang through the speaker.

"Okay, happily," she responded and hung up. She stopped what she was doing and went down out to meet him. As soon as she walked out the door she saw Rodney leaning on his car.

"Do you know me enough to ride out with me now?" he asked.

Dahlia looked up the street and saw the same group of guys standing in the same place they were the day before.

"Hey yoooo!" Rodney yelled towards the group of guys. "Me and her are gonna ride out, Imma get with y'all later." He looked at Dahlia and saw that she didn't think that was good enough. "And if anything happens to her, remember that she was with me," he added.

"I don't know what else I can say," he said, looking at Dahlia with a smile.

"They are your friends," Dahlia responded.

"Well, damn!" Rodney said. "I'm sure you know someone you can call, letting them know that you're with me. You won't be disappointed," he assured with a serious and confident expression on his face.

When he made the statement about her having a friend she could call, Dahlia immediately thought about Roro. That's the one person that she would call in situations like this. *"Damn, my girl,"* she thought, wondering who she would feel comfortable calling. She decided to call her mom. She told her mother Rodney's full name that was written on his license and gave her his license plate number.

"Okay I'm ready," she said, locking the door behind her.

After Dahlia got in the car, they stopped at the7-11.

"Do you need anything?" he asked, opening the car door.

"No thanks, but thanks though." He looked at her and smiled as if he knew she was trying to be sexy. They giggled and he went inside the store.

While he was in the store, Dahlia noticed two girls walking towards the store, staring at Rodney's car. The women looked as if they were trying to figure something out. One of the women started opening the door to the store, but she quickly turned around and headed towards Rodney's car.

"Don't do it girl," her friend begged her.

"I just wanna know," the other girl assured her friend.

The girl walked to the passenger side of the car, where Dahlia was sitting, and attempted talking to her. "Where is Red?" the girl asked.

"Who is Red?" Dahlia asked. Before the girl could respond, Rodney rushed towards his car.

"Get the Fuck away from my car!" he yelled at the woman.

"Who's that?" the girl yelled back at him, pointing at Dahlia.

"Bitch get the fuck from around my car," he yelled angrily, walking toward the driver's side. The girl ran around to the driver's side and attempted to hit him before he could get in the car. "Carry yo ratchet ass on!" he said and grabbed her arms, pushing her back.

"I hate you!" she yelled at him from the top of her lungs. "I fucking hate yo ass!"

Dahlia watched the woman as tears ran down her face. Rodney didn't seem to care. He jumped in the driver's seat and drove off.

"Who is that?" Dahlia asked him, feeling all too familiar with the situation that had just transpired. Rodney began to explain him and the girls relationship. Dahlia began to think back to her and Smoke's situation. She remembered having the same feelings and reactions as the girl in the 7-11 parking lot. She remembered the pain of knowing that her boyfriend was with another woman. She could almost still taste the salt from the tears that raced down her cheeks that day.

"Take me home," she demanded.

Rodney looked at Dahlia with disappointment, but he understood. He wasn't upset with her, but he was upset that the girl ruined his time with Dahlia. After what she had been through, that was a turn-off.

"Okay," Rodney said after a short pause. He drove up the street a little before making the first U-turn he could legally make. They drove in silence until they arrived in front of her house. When Dahlia got out of the car, she thanked him.

"Okay," he said, looking straight ahead, obviously still upset at how their night got cut short.

"Talk to you later," she said, but he never responded before driving away.

Later that night, after a long shower, Dahlia laid back on her bed. She thought of what that girl from the store probably felt after seeing her boyfriend at a store with another woman. Even though she had never seen Smoke's new girlfriend, she was still extremely hurt. She couldn't imagine ever seeing it. That had to of been a hard pill to swallow. Or maybe they had been broken up for a while, and she was too hurt to let him go. *"I don't know what it is...maybe he'll call and tell me later,"* she thought as her eyes became heavy.

"Who are you!" Dahlia yelled at the tall man as he chased her. "Why are you doing this!" She looked behind her, watching as he gained on her. He reached his hand out to grab her throat. "What the Fuck!" Dahlia yelled opening her eyes, realizing her surroundings. *"Why do I keep having these damn dreams,"* she thought to herself. She laid there for a second, staring at the ceiling. *"Oh well, let me get myself together for work."*

After a long day of work, it was nothing better than seeing Roro waiting for Dahlia at her bus stop.

"OH MY GOSH!" Dahlia yelled and ran to embrace her friend.

"Girl," Roro said, preparing to tell Dahlia the tea.

"What...bitches lying on your name?" Dahlia asked.

"Hell yeah." Roro explained everything she had been through for the last couple of days.

As they walked toward Roro's house, they walked past the same group of guys that knew Rodney. As they approached the guys, they started to yell at Roro, not even acknowledging Dahlia, as if she wasn't there. They continued walking as Dahlia began to get Roro caught up to speed with her and Rodney.

"Red, the Jamaican guy Red!" Roro yelled.

"Yeah, the Jamaican guy Red, so what? Do you know him?" Dahlia asked.

"Yeah, I know of Red, but I don't know him personally. He owns a few barbershops and that Caribbean restaurant on Princess Ann Road, amongst other things," Roro noted.

"What other things?" Dahlia questioned.

"You know, other things. Must I spell it out?" Roro asked, staring at Dahlia.

"Oh," Dahlia blurted as she finally made sense of what her friend just said. "So, he's a dope boy?"

"You know what Dahlia?" Roro looked at her from the corner of her eyes, "You're so fucking smart." They both burst out in laughter as they walked home.

Later that day, Dahlia watched as Smoke parked his car in front of her house.

"Hey, Mecca!" Dahlia yelled.

Mecca was even more excited. "Hey, Mommy!" He ran toward her and jumped in her arms.

"How was it...did you have fun?" she asked him.

"Yes ma'am," he replied. Dahlia kissed Mecca on his forehead. Smoke followed and planted a kiss on his forehead, "Bye little man." He looked toward Dahlia and walked away. Although Dahlia acted like it didn't faze her, it really did. Her eyes teared up as she carried Mecca in the house.

Later that night while Mecca was asleep, Dahlia watched music videos.

"Where my girls at, from the front to back, if you can feel that, put one hand up" she sang, when all of a sudden, the phone rang. "Hell naw," she said, upset that the phone interrupted her song.

"Hello," she answered, already annoyed at whoever was on the other end of it interrupting her vibe.

"What's up?" Rodney said.

"Oh hey," she responded, forgetting all about where her girls were at.

"Come outside," he said. She hung up the phone and went outside where Rodney had already pulled up.

"We need to talk," he said.

"We don't need to do anything, you need to talk," Dahlia clarified.

"Okay," he admitted. "WE don't need to talk then, I do." Dahlia didn't respond.

Rodney explained how him and the girl at the store had broken up and now she wouldn't leave him alone. He promised Dahlia that what happened would never happen again. Inside, Dahlia felt the situation at the store was almost a repeat of what she had just gone through, but it wasn't his fault that the girl was still hanging on. Besides, he fascinated her.

"Just call me," she said walking towards her door, not pausing to wait on a response.

"When?" Rodney asked.

"Like right now," she answered. Rodney, surprised that Dahlia gave him another chance, called as soon as he got a chance. They talked about a lot of things, including him wanting to provide classes for upcoming barbers in one of his barbershops. He even mentioned how he was thinking about selling the restaurant, but of course, he never mentioned drugs. Dahlia didn't either. The more they talked, the more interesting he became. He captivated her with his mind.

"Oh shit!" Dahlia yelled once she finally opened her eyes, noticing the phone laying by her ear without a dial tone. She fell asleep on the couch talking to Rodney on the phone. She now heard the faint sounds of her alarm clock behind a closed bedroom door.

"What time is it?" she wondered as she tried to make out the time of the clock hanging on her living room wall. "No way!" she yelled. Her shift started an hour ago. Dahlia hung up the phone and called her job. As soon as she put the phone on its hook, it immediately started ringing.

Dahlia put the phone up to her ear. Before she could say anything, Rodney spoke, "Yo, Dahlia. I've been trying to call you for hours. I know that you're supposed to work this morning. Do you need a ride?" He paused. "Or, I could pay you for today, if you don't feel like going in. But in order for me to do that, you would have to hang out with me. It's your call, I'm leaving it up to you." That sounded very tempting to Dahlia, but she couldn't accept the offer. She did, however, accept the ride. If she would've had to sit on that long ass bus ride, it most definitely would've made matters worse. After Dahlia and Mecca got ready, Rodney picked them up.

Dahlia was surprised with how Rodney interacted with Mecca. She could tell that he had a genuine love for kids.

"Thanks for the ride," she said, smiling as she grabbed her hair bag from the back seat.

"Anytime," he replied and watched as she walked inside her job.

The work day went by quickly as it typically did. Once their shifts ended, Dahlia and Roro walked out of the salon and were greeted by Rodney standing outside of the salon, leaning on his car.

"You need a ride?" he asked.

Roro decided to answer for Dahlia. "Hell yeah!"

"Of course, we do," Dahlia finally responded, also happy that they didn't have to catch the bus.

After Rodney dropped Roro and Jeremiah off, he asked Dahlia if he could take her and Mecca out to eat. She agreed, but she was even more impressed by the way Mecca gravitated towards Rodney. They both mimicked the way she ate, by holding her pinky finger out.

"Big head!" Mecca called her, knowing that it made Rodney laugh. He smiled at Dahlia as Rodney gave him different jokes to throw at her. Dahlia thought it was the cutest thing but didn't show it. She was starting to feel comfortable, the same way she felt when her and Smoke were together. After they ate, they went to the zoo and Rodney took them home.

"You can come in if you want," Dahlia said unfastening her seatbelt, not looking in his direction.

Rodney was surprised. "Okay," he replied enthusiastically and unfastened his seat belt. They went upstairs and inside her apartment. Dahlia told him to have a seat and went to put Mecca in his bed.

"Mecca finally fell asleep," Dahlia said with a sigh as she sat beside Rodney on the couch.

"Oh yeah?" Rodney questioned. Dahlia looked up at him and noticed the way he looked at her. It was a look of desire.

"What's wrong?" she asked as if she was concerned.

"Nothing, what's up with you?"

"I don't know," she answered. "Just going with the flow of things, you know."

"What's up with you?" she asked.

"You," he answered.

"What about me?" She couldn't dismiss the look of desire on his face when she sat beside him.

"I'm interested in knowing you."

"Wow," she thought, she was expecting him to say something else. Dahlia felt like she knew too well what

that look meant. *"Maybe he's different. Most guys would have been trying to talk their way into my bedroom by now."*

"Well, what is it you wanna know?" she asked.

"Everything."

"I don't know you like that," she responded in a repulsed tone.

Dahlia began to reminisce on the breakup between her and Smoke. She remembered answering the phone this particular day.

"Hello?" she said into the phone.

"Hello," the female voice with a heavy accent answered.

"Can I help you?" Dahlia asked.

"Yes," the unfamiliar voice answered.

The woman went on to tell Dahlia how her and Smoke had been in a relationship for months now and he was leaving Dahlia for her. Before Dahlia could respond she heard someone say hello again. This time it was Smoke. Dahlia's heart felt like it was being pulled out of her chest, leaving an empty space. She could hear the female in the background yelling things to her, that there was no way she could've known, unless, unless Smoke had told her. That was a major shocker because she thought him, of all people, was someone that she could trust. Now her deepest secrets laid in the hands of some strange woman that she didn't even know.

"By the way," that bitch yelled, and with all of her might, began to spew anything she could to over-talk Dahlia. Dahlia already knew what her plan was. Her only aim was to hurt Dahlia. She was going to start by revealing whatever information Smoke revealed to her. Then spilling whatever beans, whenever she felt like it. Dahlia felt violated. Smoke had literally betrayed her. Never again would she put all of her trust, especially her deepest secrets, with anyone except Roro.

Dahlia looked at Rodney, this time looking sad. "Well, I don't know about everything."

"I want to know what makes you sad," he responded as if he dived into her energy. She looked at him with a smile while laying her head on his shoulder. "I can make it better," he continued. Dahlia didn't respond, and he knew that he needed to say no more. He wrapped his arms around her, and they were silent for the rest of the night. It was comforting to her. After all of the pain she had been through lately, it felt unreal.

Rodney seemed so genuine with no ulterior motives. He didn't try to rush anything, just took his time, as if he had it in abundance. He held her all night, and the feeling of protection was undeniable. The next morning when she woke up, he was getting up and getting dressed when he noticed her staring.

"I'm taking you to work," Rodney said as he leaned down and kissed Dahlia on the forehead.

"Okay," she replied. "What time is it?" She looked at the clock, it was still early enough for her to fix breakfast and relax a little before work.

"I'll be back," he said, walking toward the door to leave.

"Okay." She got up, gave him a hug and he left.

"How did we fall asleep like that? I'm slipping," she mumbled as she grabbed the toast from the toaster. After Dahlia got herself together, she looked out the window to see Rodney already outside waiting on her. She grabbed her bag and ran to the car. As they pulled off, Dahlia noticed a short heavy set guy staring at Rodney's car. *"Maybe he knows him,"* she thought as they passed the guy. She looked at Rodney and noticed that he also was looking at the guy, and neither him nor the strange guy spoke to one another. They both stared at each other. It was obvious that they acknowledged each other but the vibe Dahlia got was uncomfortable.

"That was eerie," she said after they passed the mysterious guy.

"You don't have to worry about anything," he said without looking in her direction.

"What do you mean by that?"

Rodney looked at Dahlia and instantly understood him without him saying a word. She would never bring that conversation up again.

***

"Hey, bitch!" Roro said to Dahlia as she and Jeremiah got in the car.

"Hey, whore," Dahlia responded. "Hey, Jeremiah."

"Hi," he responds, hiding his face in Roro's arm.

Dahlia loved him as if he were her own, and Roro felt the same about Mecca. *"If I ever make it, they wouldn't have to worry about nothing,"* she thought. She turned around to see Rodney staring at her.

"Are you okay?" he asked with a smile.

"Yeah, I'm fine," she responded, simultaneously daydreaming of Jeremiah and Mecca in her huge back yard playing on their swings—a treehouse they could go to and escape from her and Roro.

"It'll be okay," Rodney assured.

"You don't even know what I'm thinking," she said.

"I don't have too. Whatever it is, it'll be okay."

For some reason, Dahlia believed him. "I hear ya."

To Dahlia's surprise, that was the beginning of Rodney taking her and Roro to work every day. The bus was now a thing of the past for them.

"What's up, Roro?" Dahlia asked as Roro and Jeremiah got in the car.

"Nothing, girl. I hope we get busy today."

"Uh bitch when aren't you busy?" Dahlia replied sarcastically with a smile.

"Why are y'all working there?" Rodney interrupted. "Why can't you just let me give you your own shop?"

"Wait a minute, what the what?" Roro asked as if she couldn't believe what she was hearing.

"Yeah, talk to your friend," Rodney said to Roro. "She won't let me put her in her own shit. For some reason, she enjoys making other people rich."

Roro looked at Dahlia in disbelief. "Bitch! Are you fucking kidding me?"

Dahlia didn't respond, she just smiled. She knew her reasons. After what she went through with Smoke, there was no way anyone would be able to take anything from her again. Everything she got she would get on her own. Her hard work, blood, sweat, and tears. Rodney dropped them off and they went to their stations and got through another long work day. When Dahlia and Roro got off, Rodney was outside waiting.

Before picking up the kids at daycare, they stopped at the gas station. When Rodney walked inside, Dahlia turned up the radio. "Oh hell naw, this is my shit! I'm slipping, I'm falling, I can't get up," her and Roro sang to DMX's song. Dahlia could see someone standing in her peripheral. It was the same girl from the 7-11 parking lot.

The girl never said anything, she just stood there staring at Dahlia, almost as if in a trance.

"Tea?" Roro asked, questioning if she knew the girl. The girl looked in the backseat as if she remembered Roro's voice.

"Roro," she replied.

"What's going on?" Roro responded, getting out of the car.

"Damn she knows her," Dahlia thought as she opened the door to get out of the car with Roro. As they approached, the girl looked at Dahlia.

"So, are you and Red together now?" she asked.

"Get the Fuck away from my damn car," Rodney hollered as he quickly walked towards them. This time the girl didn't budge. It was as if she didn't hear him, her eyes stayed fixated on Dahlia.

"Yes, we are," Dahlia responded, interested in what Tea had to say.

"What's up?" Roro asked again. Roro looked at Dahlia and immediately remembered Dahlia telling her about the situation she had at 7-11.

"What the fuck is going on...you used to Fuck with Red too?" Roro asked Tea.

"That's the guy that I was telling you about," Tea responded.

Dahlia looked at Roro confused. "You know her?"

"Yeah, she's Jason's cousin Tea," Roro said.

Rodney anxiously reached the car. "Let her speak," Dahlia said before he could tell the girl to leave again. Dahlia really wanted to hear her out. Why was she so sad? What hasn't Rodney told her? What was he hiding?

The girl began to tell Dahlia how her and Red were in a relationship, and he constantly cheated. She began to say something else but stopped herself as if in mid thought. Dahlia looked at Rodney as he put his head down, trying not to make any kind of eye contact.

"Good luck on changing a no good ass nigga," she said, staring at Rodney. She turned to Roro, gave her a hug, and as fast as she appeared, she was gone. Dahlia watched the girl walk away. She identified with that pain.

"Let's go." She opened the car door and got in, and the others followed. They left the parking lot, but Tea was still on Dahlia's mind the whole ride home.

Dahlia and Roro talked about the situation, way after Rodney dropped them off.

"Man, what's up with that?" Roro asked.

"Girl, your guess is as good as mines," Dahlia responded.

"Watch that shit," Roro said, looking Dahlia directly in the eyes.

"I got ya." Dahlia understood what Roro was saying. The situation had red flags, all over it. *"But maybe he had a good explanation,"* she thought, wanting to give him the benefit of the doubt. "I guess time will tell."

"Seriously though, Dahlia...watch that nigga. I know Tea, and she cool as shit."

"I told you that I heard you, with yo talking ass," Dahlia responded as she picked up a pillow from the couch and hit Roro with it.

"Little bitch!" Roro said laughing, catching the pillow before it hit her.

"Anyway, what's up with Jason and his flunky?" Dahlia asked.

"Them bitches quiet, and I don't trust that shit," Roro responded.

"Has he checked on Jeremiah?" Dahlia asked warily.

"Nothing bitch.... Nothing for his son. I haven't seen Jason since the night at the club. I think he feels like a BIOTCH after that knock out...do you think my shoe print is still on that ass?" Roro joked.

"I can't with yo ass," Dahlia said as she stood up. "Let's go sit on the porch." They walked out to the porch and had a seat.

"Is that Mr. Chris?" Dahlia yelled at an older man walking up the street pushing a grocery cart.

"Yes, it's me," he replied walking towards her and Roro. Mr. Chris was an older man that would use his grocery cart to get groceries for the single women in the neighborhood that didn't have a car. All you had to do was write out what you wanted and have his 40 ounce when he returned. Dahlia grew to like Mr. Chris. She kind of felt sorry for him.

"Bitch, why you call him over here?" Roro asked.

"Shut the fuck up!" Dahlia said walking towards Mr. Chris.

"Hey, Mr. Chris. What's up homie?" she asked and gave him a hug.

"You need something from the store?" he asked.

"Nope, but I got a few dollars for you," she responded, handing him a ten dollar bill. His eyes lit up as he stared at the money.

"What's that for?" he asked, confused.

"It's for you being you," Dahlia responded.

"Thanks," he said and U-turned around to walk to 7-11. Dahlia walked back to the porch where she left Roro.

"Look at this shit," Roro said looking at Mr. Chris. "He was walking slow a few minutes ago."

Dahlia looked at Mr. Chris as he powerwalked to the store. She looked at Roro, "Bitch," she said, and they both laughed.

Though Dahlia laughed, she understood how things could change in an instant. She never judged him in that way. As far as she was concerned, he had to deal with his own demons, just like the rest of us. Who was she to look down on him because of how he dealt with his pain.

While Dahlia and Roro watched Mr. Chris walk to the store, they saw his friends all gather with him to walk to the store. They wanted to share that one 40 ounce.

"See, now he's ass backwards," Roro said glancing at Dahlia and quickly turning her attention back to Mr. Chris and his group of friends. "He supposed to drink that 40 by himself."

"Where is he gonna go Roro?" Dahlia asked. "He has nowhere to go."

"Well damn, how about your house bitch! Aren't you captain save a hoe?"

"Fuck you!" Dahlia said laughing. "You're an evil bitch."

"You damn right," Roro responded proud. But Dahlia knew the real Roro. She also knew the reason she said that he was supposed to drink alone. Whenever Mrs. Pat would go to church, Roro would let Mr. Chris come in and drink his 40, just so he could enjoy it alone. They watched him and his friends until they were out of sight.

"They gone kill that 40," Roro told Dahlia laughing.

"Bitch it's already dead." They both began to laugh again.

***

Dahlia was off for the next few days, so she decided to make it all about Mecca.

"You want to go to the park?" she asked.

"Yeah," he yelled. It was his favorite place. With most kids, it would be the swings, sliding board or something like that, but not for Mecca. It was the time he spent with his mother. Dahlia knew it, even at the young age of three.

Dahlia and Mecca laid in the grass at the park and watched the stars. Dahlia, again, began to think about her grandfather. She remembered when she was around Mecca's age, watching her first, what she thought as a 3 year old, horror movie, King Kong. She remembered hiding behind her grandpa on certain scenes and loved the way he made her feel protected. She also thought back on the relationship him and her grandmother had. *"Beautiful,"* she thought as she smiled.

CHAPTER 3

Tropical Depression

I bet you can't find the big dipper," Dahlia said to Mecca. Mecca pointed towards the big dipper, remembering from the last visit. "You are so smart." She kissed him on the forehead. "Let's go." She packed up the blanket, and they headed home.

As they walked to the house, she noticed Smoke parked in front.

"Hey," he said as they walked up. "Can he go with me?"

Dahlia looked down at Mecca with a smile. "Let me get his things." Dahlia didn't invite him in. Instead, she left Mecca outside to entertain his father while she packed his things.

When she finished and opened the door, Smoke was already standing at the door and Mecca was in the car.

When Smoke snatched Mecca's belongings from Dahlia, she knew something wasn't right. *"What could've happened that fast,"* she thought. Before she could ask, he turned around and walked away. Dahlia went back in the house, wondering what was on his mind when the phone rang.

"Hello," Dahlia said, answering the phone after the first ring.

"Hey...what's up?" Rodney said.

"Hey you." Dahlia was excited to hear his voice.

"What are you doing?" he asked but didn't wait on her response. "I'm coming over." Dahlia agreed, she enjoyed talking to him and wanted him to bombard her day. Rodney had to have been somewhere close by, because after only a few minutes, he was in front of her house.

Rodney stood on her porch, waiting on her to come outside. The closer she got to him, she noticed an unsettling look on his face.

"What's up?" she asked.

"Lock your door and ride with me," he suggested.

Dahlia locked her front door and jumped in the car with Rodney. He stopped at a few houses, while Dahlia sat in the car listening to music. After stopping at one of the houses, Rodney asked her if she had any plans later that day.

"Naw...why?"

"I have something to do right quick but wanted to come back later and chill with you," he said after pulling up in front of her house.

"Okay, you can stop by later," she said as she got out of the car.

While Dahlia fumbled with the lock trying to get inside her door, she could hear her phone ringing. When she finally unlocked the door, she ran and grabbed the phone.

"Hello!" she quickly answered, trying to catch her breath at the same time. *"Damn, they hung up,"* she mumbled.

She hung up but as soon as she turned to walk away, it immediately rang again.

"Hello," she answered.

"Who the fuck is around my son?" Smoke yelled from the other end.

"What are you talking about?" Dahlia asked confused.

"So, you got some other nigga around my son?" Smoke asked. Who are you talking about... Rodney?" Dahlia asked.

"Why is he around my son?" Smoke yelled, cutting her short before she could finish what she was saying.

"The same reason your girlfriend is around my son," she responded sarcastically. She heard a pause, followed by the dial tone in her ear.

When Dahlia's phone hung up, she thought about her and Smoke's breakup, remembering the first day she heard about his new girlfriend. That particular day Smoke had taken Mecca out with him for the day, which was very rare.

When Smoke and Mecca came home that night, Dahlia asked Mecca did he have fun spending time with his dad.

"Yes mommy," Mecca answered, still excited.

"Daddy and Miss Em, took me to the zoo." Dahlia immediately looked at Smoke, "Miss Em?" She asked Smoke who was caught off guard. Smoke didn't respond, he just walked away. Dahlia walked closely behind him.

"Who in the hell is Mrs. Em?" she repeatedly yelled. "Tell me who Em is!" Instead of answering her, he locked himself inside of Mecca's room and slept in there that night.

"That motherfucker got all the nerve," she thought, slowly coming back to reality and walking away from the phone. *"What in the Fuck can he possibly have to say about Mecca being around anyone that I'm dating. At least I waited until we broke up."*

When Rodney picked Dahlia and Roro up from work the next day, he was extremely quiet. Dahlia didn't let that affect her mood. She kept talking to Roro, not giving him

Inspire wise

any inkling that she was feeding his silence. Although she secretly was wondered what was on his mind.

After Rodney dropped Roro off, Dahlia finally decided to ask him if he was okay.

"I'm cool," he answered, acting is if he wasn't in the mood to engage in further discussion. Dahlia didn't want to seem pushy, but she knew that something was wrong.

"Okay," she said, "you just seem a little distant."

Rodney looked at Dahlia in a way that made it clear to her what he was thinking. *"Leave me the fuck alone and let me think!"* He had opened up to her about a few things, but he would also often say things like, "You couldn't handle what's on my mind." Or... "It's some things I'd prefer to keep to myself, to protect me and you." So, she didn't say anything else to him, she just sat back in her seat and looked out the window the entire ride home. When Rodney pulled up in front of Dahlia's house, Rodney finally decided to say something.

"I'll talk to you later," he said. She nodded and watched her get out of the car. As soon as she closed the car door, he drove off quickly.

Later that night, Dahlia decided to watch a little tv while she waited on Rodney to call. Her eyes became heavy and before she knew it, she was at her job counting money. The atmosphere felt different, for some reason. She wondered why she was at work in the middle of the night alone. Usually that would never happen. There is no way that she would be at no one else's business alone in the middle of the night, risking her life, to count their money. All of a sudden, Dahlia heard the bathroom door of the salon slam. She looked up to see that the same tall man was in the salon and aggressively coming towards her.

He didn't give her the chance to run before he placed his hands around her throat and started to squeeze her neck.

"Help!" Dahlia tried to yell. "Help me!" But she was yelling in vein. No one was in the salon, let alone the entire shopping center that late at night. It was just her and him.

Dahlia heard a knock on the salon door. She opened her eyes and immediately felt relieved, before jumping up. *"Why do I keep dreaming about this guy?"* she asked herself. Dahlia again heard someone knock on her door. She got herself together, and nervously looked out the peephole. Boy was she happy to see Rodney standing outside her door.

"Hey," she said smiling, opening the door inviting Rodney inside.

"Hey" he responded. "What are you doing?" he asked, letting her lead the way to her living room.

"Nothing...just watching tv." They both sat on the couch. Rodney grabbed the spare blanket draped across the couch, not wanting to interrupt whatever it was that she was watching before he got there.

Dahlia felt safe with him there. She moved closer to him as he embraced her, and felt an urge to hold her tighter.

The way he held her was different than how Smoke did.
Not that Smoke never held her, this just felt warmer, and
genuine.

The closer their bodies got, the more Dahlia began to
overthink. One thought saying...' *Girl go ahead...have
some fun. You are single and Mecca is gone."* While the other
thought said..."*No you better not...you don't know him like
that."*

As the two thoughts fought against each other, Dahlia
herself, started fighting, trying to distinguish the
differences between the good thought, and the bad one.
Only one of them could win, and Rodney was feeling real
good right now, as she laid safely in his arms. That night
she finally came to a conclusion. She decided that
Rodney was worth it, so she gave herself to him. She felt
as though it was everything she expected. As she gave
him all of her stress and heartache, he in return gave her
a feeling of safety and peace.

That night Dahlia slept with her window up. When she
woke, she could hear her neighbors outside talking. The

more she listened, she noticed they were talking about her.

"She doesn't look as good as she used to," one of the men said.

Another added, "Yeah, when she first moved around here, she did look better."

"Man, that girl still looks the same," another said.

"Well, she still fucking her baby daddy!" her neighbor said.

Dahlia couldn't believe it, and immediately woke Rodney up. She wanted him to witness, and hear the men outside gossiping about her. His response though, wasn't what she expected.

"Who gives a fuck what they think," he responded, annoyed that she even cared. "What do those niggas do for you, better yet, how are they benefiting you?"

Dahlia was still upset. "I'm just not fucking with them no more," she said. Even though Dahlia knew what Rodney said was real, she was still upset. "I'm just not fucking with my neighbors anymore."

"It's your choice." Rodney turned his back, hoping the conversation was over, so he could continue sleeping. "You go ahead and keep losing sleep over a people that pay none of your damn bills. Go back to sleep, with yo sleepy ass." He laughed.

"Shut up!" she yelled, then laughed as she laid her head on his back.

As Dahlia laid in bed, she started to notice how quickly time began to fly by. She would have to get ready for work soon. She didn't want to budge, it felt so good laying next to Rodney, but she knew she had to get dressed. She already knew what it felt like, by letting a guy take care of her, which left her in the predicament that she was in now. She didn't want to relive that again.

"Let me get my ass up," she said sighing.

"Don't get up, stay here with me today," Rodney said.

Even though it sounded good, she knew that she couldn't. "I have to pay my bills, they won't pay themselves."

"How about this," Rodney proposed. "I'll pay you for a day's work today."

Dahlia never really called out and started to rethink whether she should call out or not, just this one time.

"Just tell them that you don't feel good," Rodney said noticing that Dahlia's wheels started turning from the look on her face.

"What if they ask me for a doctor's note?" Dahlia questioned.

"You're putting too much into it," Rodney said. "Who in the fuck goes to the doctor every time they feel a little sick?"

Dahlia wanted to chill, but Roro was at home, probably waiting on her. "But what about Roro? Can we still drop her off?"

Dahlia could tell that Rodney was probably secretly thinking "What about her?" She knew that his main purpose of not wanting her to go in today was because he didn't want to get up.

"Yeah, we can do that, I'm hungry anyways," he admitted.

Dahlia was really feeling this. She could get paid for chillin' at home with a guy that she was interested in. "Okay, let me call out."

After they dropped Roro off across the street from the job, they stopped at a restaurant and ate breakfast. After breakfast, they rode around, listening to music and talking. He stopped at a few houses, before eventually ending back at her house.

When they pulled in front of the house, Dahlia saw the same neighbor that was talking about her, standing in front of the house with a few other men. He looked at Dahlia and Rodney, "What's up?" he said.

"Nothing!" Dahlia responded, snarky and straight to the point. Rodney said nothing to him. In fact, he acted as if Dahlia's neighbor wasn't even there. When they walked in the house, Dahlia noticed something new about herself and Rodney. She was turned on by his confidence. *"Nothing like a guy that knows his place as a man,"* she thought, unlocking the door.

"The fuck you thinking about them niggas for?" Rodney asked her. The look he gave her was as if he viewed her and himself on a higher standard than them. Dahlia didn't think that she was better than her neighbor, nor anyone else for that matter. She didn't understand why people thought or said things like that. She never revealed her thoughts when people acted that way, she only smiled. But deep inside, she felt guilty for planting a fake smile on her face because she really didn't find it funny.

"Order a pizza and some wings," Rodney told Dahlia. "I forgot I have a movie for us."

Dahlia ordered the pizza and wings like he asked and waited for him to come back in with the movie.

"What's taking him so long?" she asked herself, then looked out the window. She saw him outside, talking to her neighbor. *"What are they talking about?"* she asked herself and walked toward the door. When she walked outside, her neighbor noticed her first, while Rodney searched for the movie.

"There she go!" the neighbor mumbled to Rodney.

"Hey, Dahlia!" he blurted out, as if he was happy to see her. Dahlia spoke, but didn't make eye contact, her attention was on Rodney.

"I'll be in in a minute," Rodney said, passing her neighbor the movie so he could pass it to her. The neighbor seemed thrilled to be of some assistance.

"Looking all good," her neighbor said, passing her the movie. Dahlia snatched the movie from him and walked back inside the house.

Dahlia had never seen her neighbor act like that before. He had flipped the script on her.

"Shit, I just heard his ass outside talking about me, now he's a fan?" Why the fuck is Rodney even talking to him?" she wondered.

When Rodney walked back inside, Dahlia immediately questioned him. "What were y'all talking about?"

Rodney sighed before he responded, "Man stuff." He didn't bother elaborating any further. Dahlia didn't entertain not knowing, she knew how to pick her battles, and this wasn't one. Instead, she put the movie on and cuddled with him as they talked.

Neither of them had questions about anything, including where he was staying that night. Dahlia didn't know how long this thing was gonna last. She did, however, know that she enjoyed his company, and with him, she felt safe.

That night Rodney told Dahlia something that stuck in her mind. He told her that she was always protected and even if he wasn't there physically, it didn't mean that he wasn't looking over her. He told her about one specific day that she turned the light on at a specific time. She remembered that day, because it was on one of those nights when she had one of her bad dreams.

It was all making sense to her now. He was acting weird on the same day that Smoke came to pick Mecca up. Dahlia stayed in her head about his admission. *"I don't know if this is a good or bad thing,"* she thought to herself. She never said anything to him about it. She did the same thing that she always did, she kept it to herself.

Dahlia slept hard that night, more then she had in a long time, leaving her feeling refreshed, and rejuvenated.

"Stay home!" Rodney said, again trying to convince her after feeling the bed move once she got up for work. "Why do you work to make someone else rich?"

"I have a son and bills," she responded. Dahlia had just unknowingly played right in Rodney's hands. She responded in the way that he had already calculated.

"I got you...don't you want your own?" he asked.

Dahlia ignored his attempts and finished getting ready for work. After Rodney dropped Dahlia and Roro off at work, Dahlia told Roro everything that happened the day before.

"Let me find out that Red been putting it down!" Roro said laughing.

"Shut up!" Dahlia yelled.

"This shit is real." Roro heard Dahlia but was thinking totally different. "I wish a nigga would tell me to stop working...shit, all I can say is, be careful what you ask for motherfucker! I would be a stay at home type of bitch. The house would be clean, food cooked, and every damn thing! It couldn't be me. But Red is right though, I have plans, and I don't wanna keep making this bitch richer off of my blood, sweat, and tears. I have to get my own salon." She continued.

"As far as your neighbor is concerned, he's a fucking crackhead, so he ain't thinking straight."

Dahlia wasn't expecting to hear that. "What? He's on drugs?"

"Yep, he's been out there for years," Roro answered.

Dahlia started putting the pieces together. *"Okay, so he knows Rodney is a dealer,"* she thought. "Damn!" she said, loud enough for Roro to hear. That's all she needed to say for Roro to understand her.

"Yep, you're right. Watch yourself," Roro said.

CHAPTER 4

Tropical Storm

D ahlia and Roro sat outside one of Roro's associates, Terri's, house in Diggs Park. They waited on Terri to finish making them daiquiri's, while Terri's 16 year old daughter took Mecca and Jeremiah to the park. That way they could unwind without having to yell at kids.

"Oh my, that drink looks good," Dahlia said to Terri when she passed them their drinks.

Terri never responded nor acknowledged that Dahlia said anything. Dahlia always felt that Terri seemed as if she didn't like her, but never understood why. She thought Terri was cool; she had to be in order for Roro to fuck with her. Dahlia, sometimes, would go out of her way to speak first, give Terri compliments, even engage in conversations. But none of that mattered. Terri just didn't like Dahlia and always threw her major shade. But Dahlia always tried to make it as comfortable as she could.

While they drunk daiquiris, Roro and Terri talked about a lot of things and people that Dahlia didn't know. She just sat back and listened, unable to comment. She stayed in her own lane and enjoyed her drink.

Evidently, Dahlia was chilling a little too much because Terri turned the conversation directly towards Dahlia.

"So, what's been up with you Dahlia?" Terri asked, sipping her drink.

Dahlia knew that it was something behind the question and didn't want to feed into whatever it was. "Nothing girl, just the usual."

Terri couldn't leave it there; she had an angle that she was getting at. "I heard you were dating Red now."

Dahlia wasn't at all surprised by Terri's bluntness. "Something like that. What you been up to?" Dahlia asked, taking the conversation off of her.

Dahlia never felt comfortable talking about her dating life with anyone but Roro. She knew that Roro was genuine, unlike Terri, who would lie and tell her what she wanted to hear, not what she needed to hear. Terri would've been the last person that Dahlia would let in on her life. Anything that she ever told Terri, was what she considered public information. That's the same information that the streets already knew, or something that she didn't mind the streets knowing.

Terri looked at Dahlia, knowing that she was attempting to change the subject. "I'm doing the same as you," Terri answered.

"Got ya," Dahlia said uninterested as she sipped her drink.

Terri had more questions, but before she could begin her interrogation again, Roro followed Dahlia's lead, sensing that Terri was on some bullshit.

"What's going on with you and Chad?" Roro asked Terri. It was the perfect question; Terri quickly changed the subject. She went on and on telling Roro about her and her boyfriend Chad's toxic relationship.

"Why do people that have their on issues stay so focused on someone else's?" Dahlia wondered as she listened to Terri talk.

"Can I get another drink?" Roro asked, overwhelmed with everything that she was hearing.

"Sure, do you want another one too?" Terri asked Dahlia as she took Roro's glass, looking at Dahlia's empty one.

"No thank you," Dahlia responded.

Dahlia wanted another drink but thought about all the things that Terri could've done to her drink while making it. *"I know this bitch feel a certain type of way about me, and I let her fix me a drink...I'm slipping,"* she thought to herself. Terri took Dahlia's empty glass and walked in the house with Roro walking close behind her.

"I gotta use the bathroom," Roro said to Dahlia. "I'll be right back." She turned around to look at Dahlia. Dahlia nodded and she walked away.

When Terri came back outside, Dahlia could feel an annoyance vibrating from her. Terri stayed quiet as if Dahlia wasn't there, then went and sat alone.

"What you bitches talking about?" Roro asked laughing as she came back outside.

"Fuck you," Dahlia joked, forcing them all to laugh.

"Absolutely nothing," Terri confirmed. She handed Roro her drink and attempted to start the conversation where she left off with Dahlia. Roro again, attempted to lighten the atmosphere.

"Girl what's been going on out the park?" she asked Terri.

Terri began to tell her all the latest gossip. Roro couldn't believe the amount of information that Terri had access to. "Bitch...yo' ass got to be channel 10 news, you know the whole 757 business. This is some Terri on your Side type of shit, bitch!" Roro said jokingly and burst into laughter. "What is the weather gone be like today?" Roro continued.

When Dahlia heard Roro ask about the weather, she couldn't help it—she burst out laughing. It came from out of nowhere, she didn't even feel it coming on. She pictured Terri sitting behind a desk, telling all the latest gossip of people in every ghetto in the 757, before giving everyone an update on the weather.

Dahlia eventually got control of her laughter. When she looked up, she saw Terri staring at her, with a look on her face that said, "Bitch, you really don't wanna laugh at me right now." Dahlia looked at the way Terri was staring at her.

"What?" Dahlia asked her...I couldn't help it, the shit was funny."

"You know that shit was funny. Stop trynna act hard," Roro said, again feeling the need to soften the situation.

Nothing about that subject was funny to Terri. She sipped her drink, but they could tell that she was secretly fuming that Roro had pulled her card. Roro didn't care at all though.

"Sorry to cut shit short, but after this drink, Imma have to break my girl," Roro said. "I got a lot of shit to do." She looked down at her drink and guzzled it quickly.

"Damn! Your thirsty ass!" Dahlia said. They both laughed.

"Okay girl," Terri said looking at Roro, "you can come by anytime." Roro and Dahlia left together.

As Dahlia and Roro walked to the park to get Mecca and Jeremiah, Roro shared her thoughts on Terri, "That's what you call a nosey bitch. We all need one of them in our lives."

Dahlia saw an opening to fire a shot at Roro for making her ride over there with her.

"That's because yo ass is nosey too!" Dahlia jokingly said to Roro. Dahlia understood what Roro meant though. Roro was more in the streets then Dahlia, and always kept her ears to it. She always wanted to know what was going on around the hoods, for as long as Dahlia could remember.

"Shit, I can't believe that bitch knew about me and Rodney," Dahlia said.

"What...is the shit some kind of a secret or something?" Roro asked confused at why she would say that.

"Naw bitch," Dahlia assured Roro, "it ain't no secret. But what did you tell her?" Dahlia asked, testing to see if she was the culprit.

"Hell naw, bitch!" Roro quickly answered, upset that Dahlia would let that question invade her mind, let alone spew it from her lips.

Roro went more into more detail, wanting Dahlia to understand where she was coming from. "I'm just saying that people are always gonna talk. And when they do, it means that you're somebody important to them. When motherfuckers stop talking, then you worry bitch. Because that means that you're a nobody, bitch."

Dahlia couldn't do anything but respect what Roro said. "I feel ya, but that's personal, and I don't fuck with that hoe like that. The bitch don't even like me, she's just

being nosey. Channel 10 news though?" They both burst
out laughing.

"Yeah, keep laughing," Roro said. "Terri's going to hear
that shit and come over here and whip your ass!" They
laughed even harder.

Later that night, after Dahlia got Mecca fed, bathed and
in bed, she laid in her own bed, thinking about Rodney.
She wondered how the news about them spread so fast.
She also wondered if Smoke really found out from
Mecca, or from gossip on the streets like Terri did. *"Wait
a minute, why do I even care?"* she mumbled. *"He got a girl.
It doesn't matter what he think,"* she thought rolling over
to her stomach squeezing the pillow. She thought of how
close they were getting and how good Rodney was with
Mecca. She thought about the magical sex they had. He
seemed like a good all-around type of guy. It was safe to
say she was feeling him.

Rodney was in the same street game as Smoke, so Dahlia
was already familiar with the dope boy lifestyle. Even
though Rodney and Smoke had similarities, they acted

different when it came to her. Smoke was more direct, non-emotional, and could be colder. While Rodney, from what she saw so far, could be cold, but only in the streets, because to her, he was warm and gentle.

She thought about one day when they were out riding. Rodney stopped by a group of guys standing on the corner in the Park Place area. Dahlia sat in the car looking at them get into, what seemed to be, an intense conversation.

After disagreeing with them for a few minutes, she saw one of the guys walk off, then come back with another guy. Rodney started cursing at the guy, but only in their language, and in a way where they could only understand each other. Roro watched the guy as he reached inside his coat pocket and pulled out a gun. Rodney snatched the gun from him, walked away, and jumped back in the car then peeled off. She didn't say anything, but she could tell by the way the guys acted when Rodney got out of the car that he was nobody to fuck with. Despite, once he got inside the car, you would never have known that any of that had just transpired. She liked that about him. He knew how to turn the streets on and off. Smoke didn't.

They were both patient when it came to Mecca. To her, that wasn't a competition because Mecca was Smoke's, so that kind of gave Rodney a one up. Smoke was doing what he's supposed to, while it showed how Rodney was with kids, which made him even more attractive. She continued with her mental comparison until she dozed off to sleep.

"Shit! Another day another dollar," Dahlia said as she turned the alarm clock off. She drug herself out of bed and got her and Mecca ready for the day. *"Where's Rodney?"* she wondered to herself. He had been waking her up for work since they'd been together, and now she hadn't heard from him in a couple of days.

Dahlia called Roro to tell her, just in case they have to catch the bus. She then called him in between getting her and Mecca dressed, but no answer. *"What did I do or say,"* she thought, realizing he wasn't going to pick up.

Dahlia noticed on her way to the bus stop that none of Rodney's friends hung out like they usually did. *"That's unusual,"* she thought. Her and Dahlia talked about it for the majority of the bus ride. They came up with many reasons it could be, most involved another woman.

"You know these are only assumptions, right?" Roro asked.

"Yeah, I know," Dahlia responded looking down.

"Either way, you'll be okay," Roro said and hit her on the shoulder, signaling that they reached their last stop.

That day, Dahlia was happy when the work day ended, more than any other day. She had a rough day at work, nothing seemed to go right. She also couldn't keep Rodney off her mind, so she knew that played a big part. When they arrived at the daycare to pick up Mecca and Jeremiah, she noticed Mecca's pants weren't the ones she dropped him off with.

"Mecca had a mistake," his teacher said to Dahlia and handed her a bag with Mecca's soiled pants and underwear.

"This doesn't usually happen," Dahlia says confused.

"I know, but we are all entitled to mistakes," the teacher replied with a gentle smile on her face looking at Mecca, "Ain't that right. Mecca?"

"Yes," Mecca replied smiling back. She gathered him and his things and left. Dahlia began to feel defeated; it seemed like the world was on her shoulders.

"How can so many things spiral out of control like this in one day? Is this even possible?" she wondered. She remembered the day her grandfather told her that it would be days like this and not to hang on to the negative aspects of it. To only look at the positive in any situation because they were all learning experiences. He also reminded her that the positive parts of it were taken with her and used them for positive daily change. But the negative part you leave behind. Only using it when you need to remember what not to do again. She never

understood that. It seemed impossible to her when so many things were happening back to back. All she seen was negativity, where was the positive anything? She also knew that right now, at this time, what she really needed was a hot bath and a glass of wine.

When Roro and Dahlia separated, and she got closer to her house, she noticed that she still didn't see any of Rodney's friends standing around like usual. Later that night while Dahlia and Mecca ate dinner, she heard someone knock on her door. "I'll be right back," she said to Mecca and got up from the table to see who the was at the door. *"It's Rodney,"* she assumed to herself, happily opening the door without looking through the peephole. When she opened it, it wasn't Rodney, but one of the guys that she would sometimes see on the corner that Rodney knew.

"Hi..." Dahlia said, confused, wondering why he was at her door.

"Hello, baby girl. Red will be calling you in a few minutes."

"Okay," Dahlia responded, wondering why Rodney would send someone else to her door instead of just calling her himself. *"And where has he been the last couple of days,"* she thought. Dahlia waited impatiently for the phone call, until finally the phone rang.

"Hello," Dahlia said when she answered.

"Hello," Rodney responded.

"What's going on, Rodney?" He sat silently on the phone.

"What is it?" she asked. Rodney started to speak but before he could, Dahlia attempted to cut him off.

"Dahlia!" He yelled, finally grabbing her attention, "I'm in jail."

"In jail?" she repeated. "What happened?"

"We'll talk about it later," he said, avoiding going into details about anything over the phone. Dahlia understood.

When Rodney's phone time ended, another woman spoke to Dahlia.

"Hi, Dahlia. My name is Gina. I'm Red's sister."

"Oh. Hi, Gina." She was still in shock by the news.

"Red told me where you live, is it okay if I come and talk to you tomorrow?" Gina asked.

"Sure," Dahlia answered. That night, Dahlia found it hard to sleep, so she slept in Mecca's room. Every time she wanted to cry, she would just hold him tightly as he slept instead.

Dahlia's mind began to wander back to when her and Smoke were still together. She remembered laying on the couch sleep, hearing someone bang on the door.

"Open the door, we have a search warrant!!!" Dahlia had tried waking from her dream but for some reason she couldn't open her eyes. She heard the banging on the door again, "Open the door we have a search warrant!"

This time Dahlia was able to open her eyes. She walked toward the door half asleep when she heard someone yell one last time. "Open the door we have a search warrant!" Before Dahlia could reach the door, she heard a loud bang and police bombarded her home.

"Get down!" they had yelled and slung her to the ground as they put her in handcuffs. "Who's here?" they asked, going from room to room with guns drawn.

Before she could mention her son, one of the officers directed Mecca out the room and to his mother. Shortly after, a fellow officer saw the two year old at the time move and almost shot him.

"You couldn't see that he was a baby!... Look how small he is!" she yelled at the officer, while another police officer showed her the warrant. As Dahlia read the warrant she saw where an informant revealed that it was a gun and drugs in the home.

"I understand, you have to do your job but look at how small he is. You could have killed my baby!" Dahlia told the officer. It fell on deaf ears because not one of the officers apologized or offered an explanation for the decision to point a gun at her toddler. Instead, they focused on questioning her about Smoke's whereabouts.

The police stayed in Dahlia's house for hours looking for a gun and drugs. Dahlia knew Smoke well. She knew that nothing like that would be in the house. And if a gun was involved, it would be in his possession at all times. They searched and searched, never finding what they came for. *"My son could've been dead if he had of made one small move,"* she thought, *"and no one would've cared."* While the officers searched Dahlia's condo, no one considered what Mecca could be thinking, they simply didn't care. Dahlia felt like her son, at only two years old, had been exposed to what it was being another black man in America. That incident eroded her trust, and from that point forward, she never looked at police the same again.

Dahlia pulled Mecca closer to her, as he slept. That's how she slept all night long. Dahlia didn't make it to work the next day. She felt a need to recover from the trail of bad luck that she had the day before. *"I wonder what happened with Rodney,"* she asked herself. She couldn't wait for his sister to come over to make light of the situation. Dahlia hoped that he wasn't locked up for something too bad. Although he went out of his way to make sure that her and Mecca were good when he wasn't there, she still felt safer with him being around.

"Hey, Mommy!" Mecca greeted in a raspy voice as he walked in the living room.

"Good morning, handsome," Dahlia said and gave him a big hug before she sat him on her lap. "I love you."

"I love you too, Mommy!" he responded.

"I love you more," Dahlia followed. They kept going on and on; it was one of the ways they proclaimed their love for one another. "I love you more than the sky", "I love you more than the moon", "I love you more than the stars", they would keep assuring one another until they grew tired. Dahlia enjoyed her son. Not because she had to be his mom, but because she truly enjoyed being his mommy. It felt as if they were souls, constantly following each other throughout many lifetimes. They were always meant to be, and she absolutely adored him, and him her.

After Dahlia finished preparing lunch for Mecca, she heard the phone ring. It was Rodney's sister Gina asking if it was a good time to come by. Dahlia assured it was and hung up, anticipating the visit. She really wanted to know what was going on with Rodney. She couldn't stop thinking about him and the different possibilities that could have landed him in jail. When Gina finally arrived Dahlia couldn't believe the resemblance between Rodney and his sister.

"Hi," Gina greeted as Dahlia opened the door.

"Hello," Dahlia said, "you can come in." Gina walked in Dahlia's living room and took a seat.

"So, I finally get to meet you," she said. "My brother has nothing but good things to say about you." Dahlia was pleased to hear that, especially since her feelings for him had started to grow stronger.

"Good," Dahlia said smiling.

"So let me tell you what's going on," Gina continued and told Dahlia everything that was happening.

After Gina's explanation to the real reason Rodney was in jail, Dahlia's head instantly started spinning, and her mouth flew open. She couldn't wrap her mind around what Rodney's sister had told her. The last word that his sister said to Dahlia still shocked her brain, "Murder!" Dahlia yelled.

"I know, we all feel the same way," Gina said. Gina went on to describe how the police had done a sweep. They ran up on some of the guys standing outside and even ran in some of their houses looking for Rodney. Eventually, Rodney turned himself in to stop them from bombarding their mother's house. Rodney wanted Gina to come and explain everything so she wouldn't have to listen or worry about what the streets were saying.

Dahlia couldn't believe any of what she was hearing. All she could remember was the word, "murder". She couldn't picture him committing murder. He was so gentle with her and Mecca. Gina gave Dahlia her number and told her to call whenever she wanted to talk and reminded her never to mention anything about the case over the phone, because it was more than likely tapped. She hugged her and walked out the door.

Dahlia spent the rest of the day on and off thinking about Rodney. She never expected to hear his sister utter those words. Although things were tough for her, she couldn't help but be grateful in the moment; this was another reason she believed GOD put Mecca in her life. He was only three but unknowingly there for her. He kept her away from all the bad things that crossed her mind. It was as if he was born to fill in the void of losing her grandfather, someone that she could share a mutual unconditional love with. With Mecca she could understand all the feelings that her grandfather had for her because she felt the same feelings for Mecca.

"I understand, Grandad," she said aloud as she looked toward the sky…"I understand now."

Dahlia giggled as she recalled the day that she told her grandfather that she would never love anyone as much as she loved him.

"Yes, you will. Wait until you have your own," he'd said.

"Well, I'm not going to love my kids more than you," Dahlia had responded.

"You say that now, you'll see."

Dahlia frowned and felt that he couldn't possibly understand her at the time. She was convinced that maybe he didn't really know what love felt like, because he couldn't have loved her as much as she loved him, otherwise he would understand.

Now, being a mother, she knew that he loved her more than anything. Dahlia tasted the salt from the tears that raced down her face. *"Why?"* she asked herself, then heard the phone ring. She didn't feel like answering. She just wanted to sit in her sadness alone. *"Oh shit, it could be Rodney,"* she thought and ran to the phone to answer. She was right, it was Rodney.

Dahlia and Rodney talked on the phone almost every day now. Some days he would call throughout the day. Even though he wasn't there physically, he was definitely there mentally. It made them even closer emotionally. Her and his sister went to all of his visitations and court dates. Gina also kept her in the know of what was going on about Rodney's case.

Dahlia and Gina had started to build a relationship. Dahlia even started talking to Gina about her and Rodney's relationship. Gina would take Dahlia and Roro to work on her off days or late work days, which both Dahlia and Roro appreciated.

One morning on a day that Gina was off, she picked Dahlia and Roro up as she usually did, and the conversation went towards Rodney and an ex-girlfriend. Gina mentioned to Dahlia that her and Rodney's ex were still good friends.

"How good?" Roro asked.

"Really good," Gina said.

"I mean like, going out to a party with each other every now and then? Or chilling at each other's house on a daily basis?" Roro clarified.

"I mean hanging out whenever we want, chilling at her house on a regular, and we talk on the phone probably every day."

"Oh, I feel you," Roro said and shot a look toward Dahlia. Dahlia already knew where Roro was going as soon as Roro began questioning Gina. Roro quickly changed the subject and they all talked until she dropped them off.

As soon as Dahlia and Roro got into the salon, Roro looked at Dahlia, "Bitch, fuck a ride. That bitch is sneaky yo. She is chilling with you and telling oh boys ex everything y'all talk about."

"Do you think so?" Dahlia asked, still tripping over Gina coming clean about her relationship with Rodney's ex.

"Duh!" Roro answered sarcastically. "That's something that should've been came up, so why now? It's either she slipped up and said a little too much and I caught that ass, or she done got all the information she needed from you and doesn't care if you know where she stands. Either way, it's some sneaky bullshit going on, mark my words."

Dahlia analyzed everything Roro said. Dahlia had known Roro majority of their lives and Roro was usually dead on.

"I hope you didn't tell her too much into your personal life." Roro side-eyed her.

"Hell naw!" Dahlia said quickly. Dahlia was usually a very private person, but for some reason she wasn't this time. Dahlia thought about all the days and nights she talked to Gina about her relationship. She felt stupid and played.

"Okay damn," Dahlia said to herself, but loud enough for Roro to hear. Roro didn't feel the need to say anything else. She just looked at Dahlia and shook her head.

"Haven't I taught you anything?" Roro scolded.

Dahlia couldn't respond because deep down inside she knew Roro was right. After all, she hadn't known Gina that long to be giving her insight into her and Rodney's relationship. For some reason, Dahlia felt like Gina was cool.

"If she's on some stupid shit, it'll be revealed," Dahlia said.

"It already was," Roro responded and looked at Dahlia as if she couldn't understand why she couldn't see what she was seeing. "Watch her ass, that's all I have to say." Roro looked at Dahlia again before going to let her client know that she was ready. "Don't make me have to cut me a couple of bitches."

Dahlia laughed but she knew Roro was serious. She knew Roro was a true friend and didn't give two fucks about having to prove that to anyone that wanted to test the waters.

When Gina picked them up, Roro was unusually quiet.

"Are you okay?" Gina asked Roro, as if sensing a problem.

"Naw, I'm chill," Roro responded, keeping quiet.

Gina looked in the rear view mirror to make sure, "Y'all must've been busy today?" she questioned with a smile on her face.

"Yeah," Roro answered as she closed her eyes.

"Well, what are you ladies getting into later?" she asked as she took her eyes off Roro and focused back on driving.

Dahlia knew Roro wasn't going to answer, so she did. "Nothing too much, I guess."

Dahlia felt confused, like smoke was being blown up her ass the entire time, and she wasn't feeling it. She had to figure out how she was going to play this situation. She kept quiet the whole ride home, only speaking when spoken to. She didn't want to make anything too obvious, so she kept reiterating how busy they were at work.

After Gina dropped them off, they talked about the situation for hours.

"She's a sneaky bitch," Roro said. "I've seen her kind before. You don't need to be talking to her ass."

"I know," Dahlia responded, "but she do take me to handle shit that I need to do."

"Bitch you never had a problem with riding the bus before. Let me find out that you'll sell your soul for a ride?"

"Naw," Dahlia said, feeling a need to explain. Before she could, Roro cut her off.

"I understand," Roro said, "but don't tell that bitch nothing that you don't want the world to know. I'm just saying."

"I know," Dahlia answered.

When Dahlia and Roro finally got off the phone, she thought about all of the things she told Gina. *"His ex knows too much about my relationship,"* she mumbled, *"this shit is fucking crazy. You can't trust a soul."* She opened a bag of chips and flicked through the channels on tv, trying to find a good movie. She heard a knock on the door.

"Who is it?" she yelled, not wanting to remove herself from her comfortable spot she had created on the couch.

Another knock came. "Damn, can't a bitch chill in peace?" she yelled as she walked to the door.

"Who is it?" she asked again., irritated from the lack of response when she asked who it was the first time.

"It's me," she heard the person say, "Smoke."

Dahlia flung the door opened quickly. She was shocked to see it him. "What are you doing here this late? Mecca's sleep."

"I figured that much," he said. "Actually, I needed to talk to you."

"Okay, come in," Dahlia said as she walked away from the door.

Smoke closed the door behind him and grabbed Dahlia before she could get too far out of his reach. He kissed her passionately while caressing her breast. Dahlia pulled away, a little confused.

"Why are you doing this?" she asked, wanting to run but unable. It was as if she was bound. Like she couldn't move and could only let nature take its course. She felt helpless. Smoke had his way with her that night. Dahlia felt like it was something they both needed. For her, this confirmed that she still had hidden feelings for him.

"What just happened?" she asked this time extremely confused.

"I don't know," he said, confused himself. "Look, I have to go." He glanced over at Dahlia briefly and left without saying another word.

"Wow," she said aloud. "What just fucking happened?" Her mind began to wander, and all sorts of things popped up. "Oh shit!" she says aloud. "What am I going to tell Rodney?"

CHAPTER 5

The Eye Of The Storm

D ahlia and Roro started back catching the bus to work. Dahlia still talked to Gina every now and then, but she didn't trust her anymore. The main reason was from what Roro had opened her eyes to, she couldn't sell her soul for a ride. She was fine catching the bus, it wouldn't be her first time, and probably far from the last. She didn't want to smile in Gina's face anyway, after what happened between her and Smoke that night.

"Speaking of Smoke," Dahlia thought to herself, *"I haven't seen or heard from him since that night."* She was okay with not talking to him. She felt that what her and Smoke did that night shouldn't have happened anyway. Especially seeing that they were both in relationships with other people.

Dahlia tried to put it all out of her mind. So, she shifted her focus to it being the weekend; she was excited because Mrs. Pat was watching the boys again that night. Of course, her and Roro planned to take advantage of the opportunity and release some stress.

That night after work, Dahlia got Mecca ready to go to Mrs. Pat's, then got herself dressed for her and Roro's night out. She didn't know where or what they were getting into, nor did she care. Just to be out and away from home was fine with her.

As Dahlia and Mecca walked up to Roro's house, she saw Roro already in the car.

"Yo' ass tryna leave without me?" she asked.

"Girl this motherfucker won't start," Roro replied frustrated.

"What?" Dahlia blurted out.

"Girl this shit is in the fucking way," Roro said.

"What's wrong with it?"

"Girl I don't know. Do I look like a fucking mechanic?" Roro asked sarcastically.

"Hell yeah. The way you're out here constantly trying to start something that won't start, with yo stupid ass," Dahlia responded.

"Fuck you," Roro said and got out of the car. "So, what are we going to do?"

"Damn, I don't know," Dahlia said. "I know you don't want to hang with Gina?"

"Hell fucking naw," Roro yelled, "...what about Terri?"

Dahlia looked at Roro, surprised that she would ask such a question. "Fuck you, Roro."

They knew that it would have to be one of the two with such short notice. They weighed the options—Terri it was.

"Now I got to deal with this nosey bitch," Dahlia said.

"Fuck that bitch, we getting the fuck out the house," Roro responded. It was either Terri or go home. It was really nothing for Dahlia to think about. She was grateful for

Mrs. Pat giving her a much needed break; she didn't know when that opportunity would come again.

"Okay Man, call her. Damn," Dahlia said.

Despite the last minute notice, it Terri took no time to pick them up.

"Where are we going ladies?" Terri asked excited.

"Shit, just getting out the house," Roro answered. "We don't give a fuck."

"Okay, that's what up," Terri said, even more excited.

Dahlia kept quiet; she didn't have much to say to Terri.

They pulled up at a bootlegger house in South Norfolk. When they walked in, they noticed a few people inside.

When they sat down, the man of the house told them that one of the gentlemen was going to pay for whatever drink they wanted. They thanked him and continued talking, trying to figure out where they were going that night. Dahlia could feel an energy, as if someone was watching her. She looked up and locked eyes with the same guy that was staring at Rodney's car when they rode by. He didn't say anything, just watched her. Dahlia tried to keep her mind off of him and focus on the conversation that she was having with Roro and Terri, but every time she looked up, he was still watching her. Dahlia noticed that everyone in the house drew to this guy as if he was someone important. After they finished their drinks and decided what club they were going to, Terri let the man of the house know that they were leaving, and they walked towards the car. The guy walked out shortly after them.

"Yo," he yelled before Terri could pull off. He walked over to the passenger side of the car, so Roro rolled her window down. "Why are you ladies leaving so soon?"

When he spoke, Dahlia realized he had an accent like Rodney's, only his was more distinct. Dahlia began to question whether the guy and Rodney knew each other from Jamaica or the States.

"Because we got shit to do," Roro answered sarcastically. After Roro introduced herself, they talked for a few minutes before exchanging phone numbers.

"Come on, Roro," Dahlia and Terri said rushing her so they could get back to their night. Roro gave the guy her number and he walked away from the car, but only after glancing at Dahlia one more time.

The three of them had fun that night. No drama, just clean fun. Fun that neither one of them had in a long time. Terri even warmed up to Dahlia that night, which surprised Dahlia and Roro. After Terri dropped them off, Dahlia explained to Roro what happened that day when her and Rodney seen the guy while driving past, and how he stared at them as they drove past.

"It's probably nothing," Dahlia assured her friend. "Just have to let you know, just in case."

"Just in case what?" Roro asked. "Because you know I won't hesitate to cut a nigga!"

"I know, Roro," Dahlia said laughing. "I'm trying to stop that part of the equation. You know that you need some professional help, don't you?"

"That's what they say," Roro replied.

"Girl, you're fucking crazy." Dahlia shook her head.

Dahlia and Mecca slept at Roro's house that night.

"You might as well get comfortable," Mrs. Pat told Dahlia. "You're not taking that baby out this late at night."

"I know, Mrs. Pat." Dahlia wasn't going to go back and forth with Mrs. Pat. She respected her enough and knew that it would've been a dead end situation. Everyone respected Mrs. Pat. Just like everyone knew that you wouldn't win going against her. What she says always goes. And that was it.

Dahlia really didn't want to wake Mecca up that late anyway. And she most definitely didn't want to walk home in the neighborhood she lived in. Dahlia curled up in Jeremiah's bed alongside Mecca. Jeremiah's bed was inside Roro's room, so Mrs. Pat placed Jeremiah in Roro's bed. Roro got in her bed, and they both were sleep in no time. Dahlia woke up in the same position she fell asleep in, with Mecca held close to her.

"Man, it smells good in here," Dahlia said to Roro as she awoke to the smell of bacon, and whatever else Mrs. Pat was cooking.

"Damn sholl do," Roro responded.

"I love your momma," Dahlia said.

"I love her too, and trust, she loves you too."

Dahlia already knew how much Mrs. Pat genuinely loved her. That was one thing that she didn't need confirmation about. The only thing that Dahlia didn't like, was that Mrs. Pat loved everyone. That made Dahlia jealous at times. She didn't like it when someone would tell Mrs. Pat they loved her, and she'd respond, "I love you too sweetheart." Even though Dahlia knew that she was wrong for feeling that way, she still did.

After Dahlia and Mecca ate breakfast, they walked home. Dahlia wasn't in the house no more than fifteen minutes before Rodney called.

"Hey, you," she answered once it was him and not the recording.

"Hey, what's up?" he responded. "I called you all last night. What… you stayed out or something?"

"Um yeah," Dahlia said. She thought it was cute that he seemed a little jealous. She told him how much fun she had with the girls last night, and that she stayed at Roro's house.

"Oh yeah," she said, "I almost forgot. Do you remember that guy, that was staring at us when we rode by?"

"Yeah, what about him?" Rodney asked.

Dahlia filled him in about how he had been looking at her at the house and how he gave Roro his number.

"Oh yeah?" he said, then dropped the subject. He didn't say anything about the situation, leaving Dahlia wondering whether she should've mentioned it. *"Maybe it's nothing to it,"* she thought.

The next day when Dahlia and Roro were on their way to work, Roro told Dahlia the guy called her. Talking to Roro, she found out that the guy's name was Jay and that he ran the house they were at that night. So far, Roro thought the guy seemed chill.

"I don't know too much about him though, still trying to figure him out. Did you mention it to Red?" Roro asked.

"Yeah I did, but he didn't mention anything. Maybe it's nothing to it," Dahlia responded.

"Maybe not, but I'm still gonna watch his ass," Roro replied.

When Dahlia and Roro got off, they noticed that a few more of Rodney's friends were back on the corner. "The boys are back," Roro said.

"I see," Dahlia responded. "I wish it was mine."

"Girl, give it some time. He'll be home soon," Roro said, trying to keep her optimistic.

"I know." Dahlia prayed what Roro said was true. All Dahlia could think about was the word murder. Dahlia didn't know too much about the law, but she knew enough to know that that charge in itself was serious.

When Dahlia and Mecca got to her house, she noticed Gina's car parked in front of her house. *"What is she doing here?"* Dahlia wondered. As she walked up Gina got out of her car.

"Hey," Dahlia said smiling.

"Hey," Gina spoke back.

"What's going on?" Dahlia asked, without asking what she really wanted to say, which is why the fuck are you here! She didn't want to come off to harsh because she didn't know for sure if Gina was on some funny shit for real.

"Nothing's up girl, just checking on you, making sure that you're okay. Do you need to go anywhere?"

"No, I'm cool," Dahlia said. "Me and Roro went shopping the other day. Do you want to come in?" she asked, hoping she would say "hell no". But Gina took her up on her offer.

"Yeah, I can stay for a few," Gina said.

"Me and my big ass mouth," Dahlia thought.

147

"What you been up to?" Gina asked.

"Nothing really." Dahlia wasn't giving up any extra information.

"I heard you went over Jay's house the other night. Did y'all have fun?" Gina asked.

"How did you know that?" Dahlia asked, but almost knowing that Rodney had to tell her. It was no coincidence to her that she had told Rodney the previous night that she went over there and Gina popped up the day after. "Rodney told you that?"

"No, he's my homegirl's brother."

Now Dahlia was really confused. She didn't understand how or why her name would even come up. What would've made Jay even mention her to Gina's homegirl? She didn't even know he knew her name.

"Who's your homegirl?" Dahlia asked Gina.

"Do you remember Rodney's ex that I was telling you about? Well, that's his sister," Gina answered.

"Oh!!" Gina thought. Dahlia now understood why the guy looked at her and Rodney as they drove by. She also understood why he stared at her the way he did that night.

"Okay, got ya...it makes a lot of sense," Dahlia said. Dahlia didn't know how to take any of this. *"What type of shit are they on, and why didn't Rodney tell me this when we talked?"* she wondered. *"And why would she feel the need to come all the way to my house, to ask me something that she could've asked me over the phone?"* Dahlia didn't know what was going on, but she knew it didn't feel right. She now questioned Gina and Rodney's motives even more.

Gina stayed and talked to Dahlia for a little while, then left. As soon as she did, Dahlia called Roro and filled her in.

"What do them motherfuckers got going on...and what type of shit did you get me into?" Roro asked jokingly. "Wait until I tell momma that yo ass ain't so holy and thou. That you finally got me into some bullshit."

"What? I told yo ass!... and I didn't tell you to take his number, nor did I push it down your throat," Dahlia said.

"Yeah, but after I got the number, it didn't matter," Roro said. "Them bitches got shady shit going on."

"I know," Dahlia said. "I just don't like the fact that I'm in the middle of the shit with a damn blindfold on. And I feel like Rodney shouldn't have put me in a vulnerable situation."

"You right. He shouldn't have put you it. Don't say shit about it when you talk to him. And please, whatever you do, don't be a pussy about it."

"Hold up, pussy about it?" Dahlia laughed.

"Yeah, we all know that you have pussy tendencies." They both laughed. They refused to stay in that energy. They just knew that they had to watch them.

That night when Rodney called her, she never mentioned anything about his sister coming over. Nor did she mention anything about the guy Jay. She wanted to see if he was going to say anything. Rodney talked about the things he wanted to do when he got out of jail. He talked about memories that he had about of him and her. He even talked about Mecca. But he still never said anything about Jay or his sister, Dahlia couldn't understand why. She hated that she felt that way about him, but he had her severely confused. He'd better come clean, and very soon.

Dahlia sat by the window and looked at the stars as she thought about everything she was going through at the time. She remembered being a young child playing in the living room one day. Her grandma and grandfather were in the kitchen. Dahlia's grandma had been extremely religious. Her grandma was playing a gospel song called "I'm going away". Dahlia had heard that song many times, but for some reason, at that young age, she was hearing it more clear. Dahlia began to picture what it would be like if she lost her grandfather, for the first time she was understanding the concept of death.

Dahlia had begun to cry. "What's wrong?" her grandparents had asked as they ran from the kitchen to comfort her. That day was Dahlia's first time for a lot of things. Dahlia couldn't phantom the heart to say what she really had thought about, so for the first time, she lied. Dahlia carried that guilt with her until this day because a few years later, her grandfather really did die. She somehow felt like if she had of told them, he would still be here today.

While Dahlia looked out the window, she saw Gina's car as it pulled up.

"What the fuck do she want now?" Dahlia thought, rolling her eyes. As the car got closer, Dahlia realized someone else was in the car. Once the car was right in front of the house, she noticed that it was another female. Dahlia watched while Gina and the other female stared at her house. *"I know that this bitch ain't riding past my house with Rodney's ex,"* Dahlia said aloud but talking to no one but herself.

CHAPTER 6

Storm Surge

H ey, Jane," Dahlia greeted her favorite client. Jane sat in her chair and let out a big sigh.

"Hey, my girl," she said to Dahlia. "I still have a house waiting on you."

"I know," Dahlia responded, "...when I'm ready, you know that I'm coming straight for you."

"Okay now, I'm going to hold you to that."

"Do that," Dahlia said as she started to comb through her hair. "What have you been up to?" Jane told Dahlia about all the fun and exciting things that she had been doing.

"What…a cruise?" Dahlia asked. "I've never been on one before." Jane explained how many things you could do on the ship alone, and all the different countries she'd been too. Jane and her husband were always doing something exciting, and Dahlia loved to hear about it all. She could see herself living in the way that Jane was, she just didn't know when or even how. But for the time being, she lived vicariously through Jane.

Later that day Dahlia and Mecca were playing hide and seek in the house as they usually did. She always knew where to find Mecca because he always hid in the same place. It was under her bed. It was easy to spot him because he never put his legs and feet fully under the bed. Dahlia, on the other hand, would hide in different places, making it hard for him to find her. She hoped that it would make him think of other places to hide, but it never did. Still, Dahlia always acted as if she couldn't find or see him. "Mecca!" she would call. "Where did he hide this time?" she would ask aloud. One day she got a phone call while he was hiding under the bed, with his legs and feet out. She almost forgot that they were playing.

"I'm right here, Mommy!" he yelled.

"Oh, I got to go," Dahlia said as she quickly hung up the phone. "I'm happy you said something," she said to him. "Because I would have never found you."

"I'm a good hider," he said as he hugged her.

"You are," she said and hugged him tight..."and you're also mommy's big boy."

There was a knock at the door. She let go of Mecca.

"Who is it?" Dahlia asked and walked toward the door.

"It's Smoke," she heard him say. Dahlia wanted to make sure that she heard it right, because she hadn't heard from Smoke since that night they had sex.

"Smoke," he yelled. "It's Smoke."

Mecca heard his Dad's voice. "Daddy," he yelled and ran to the door.

"What did I tell you about opening the door?" she scolded him.

"But mommy, it's daddy," Mecca explained.

"I don't care if it was Jesus!"

"Because he wouldn't knock on the door, he would just appear." Mecca looked at Dahlia like he didn't understand what she was talking about.

Dahlia opened the door to see Smoke standing there with some kind of bag in his hand. He looked at her as if he wanted to say something.

"Daddy!" Mecca yelled as he ran and jumped in his father's arms. Smoke picked Mecca up and hugged him. When Smoke told Mecca that he loved and missed him, Dahlia rolled her eyes, but only when Smoke would look at her.

"Play hide and seek with us, Daddy," Mecca demanded.

Smoke looked at his son, still holding him in his arms, "You're mommy don't like me, so she doesn't want me to play."

Mecca and Smoke turned around to a wide eyed confused looking Dahlia. Smoke laughed at the look Dahlia had on her face, which only irritated her more.

"Mecca you get to spend time with your dad. He's better at playing games than me," Dahlia said as she mouthed "I hate you" to Smoke. She left the two to bond and walked to her bedroom. Dahlia laid across her bed and painted her nails when she heard her phone ring. She jumped up to answer the phone. As Dahlia entered the living room, she saw that Smoke had answered her phone. "Who is that?" Dahlia asked. Smoke never responded, just stood in silence with the phone to his ear. She wondered why he would even answer the phone.

"Who's that?" she asked Smoke again, this time trying to grab it from him. Smoke turned away from her so she couldn't grab ahold of the phone.

"Give me my fucking phone," Dahlia yelled frustrated.

Smoke had one purpose only, and that was to find out who was on the other end of the phone. "What's up Red?" Smoke said, this time finally looking at Dahlia. "Long time no hear from."

"You know him?" she asked. Smoke was so caught up in the conversation, he didn't hear her. He didn't say too much, mostly just listened to Rodney. Smoke seemed to have been angered by something Rodney said. "Just stay the fuck away from my son." Smoke hung up.

"How do you know him?" Dahlia asked, confused at the conversation. "...and you have a female around my son on a regular, why can't I have a man?" she asked him. Ignoring her, he grabbed Mecca and walked out the door.

"Ask him," he finally answered as he walked toward the car.

"Where are you going with my son?" Dahlia asked, not understanding what just happened.

Smoke never looked back at Dahlia, "I'm taking my son with me." Without hearing or even caring about a response from Dahlia, he put Mecca in the car and drove off.

Dahlia waited for Rodney to call. Being that she couldn't get a response from Smoke, maybe Rodney could. She wanted to know what Rodney said on the phone to make

Smoke mad enough to take their son, and how they even knew each other.

"This was too much," she thought and walked back into the house. She was starting to feel exhausted with both relationships from Rodney and Smoke. *"Maybe it's a man thing,"* she said to herself. *"Could it be me?"* Dahlia reminisced over her and Smoke's relationship, from the beginning to the end. Then did the same to her and Rodney's, looking for anything that she could think of. Both Smoke and Rodney were holding secrets from her, and she was determined to find out why. Dahlia fell asleep that night waiting on a call that would never come.

For some reason, getting up or even dressed for work that morning seemed to be too much. Mecca stayed with Smoke many nights, but this time it felt different. It was the first time she didn't have a choice. Dahlia was so deep in thought about everything that had happened that she missed the bus, which made her an hour late for work.

That in return made her work day more hectic. It seemed like the work day just drug along.

"Girl you can't let them take over your mind," Roro said to Dahlia as they walked towards Roro's house after work. "Maybe Smoke really didn't know Red, he probably heard Mecca speaking about him and felt some type of way."

"No Roro," Dahlia began to explain, "Smoke specifically said that they haven't heard from each other in a while. That, to me, says that they have some type of history."

Roro thought about what Dahlia said and agreed. "You're right, but why lie?"

"That's what I want to know."

They arrived to Roro's and discussed all the possibilities of Dahlia's situation. Later that night, when Dahlia left Roro's house, she noticed that the majority of Rodney's friends were back on the block. The closer she got the more they stared at her. That irritated her, because she never understood how a person can stare at a person and not speak.

"Hello," she spoke as she reached them.

"Hello," they all spoke back. She just kept walking, but she could feel their eyes beaming on her from behind. She wondered what they were thinking and if they knew what happened between Rodney and Smoke. *"Who cares, they never really spoke to me anyway,"* she reminded herself as she walked inside the house.

Dahlia waited again for a call from Rodney. The later it became, she came to the realization that he probably would never call again. She would more than likely never know what was said over the phone because Smoke most definitely wasn't going to tell her. *"What kind of a relationship is this?"* she thought as she plunged onto her bed. *"Why do it have to be such a secret?"* she thought to herself. She couldn't tell if Smoke was acting like this because he was jealous that she was finally beginning to move on, or if it some bad blood between the two. As she laid on her bed deep in thought, she heard a knock on the door.

"That must be Smoke bringing Mecca back," she thought as she ran to the door. It took her by surprise to see Gina standing outside of the door with a woman she had never seen before, looking her up and down.

"Hey girl," Gina said as if she was happy Dahlia opened the door.

"Hello what's up?" Dahlia asked then invited them in with arm wave. Dahlia felt uneasy about this. Gina never came to Dahlia's house without calling first. She led the way to her living room. "Have a seat." She sat down and waited for them to get to the point.

"What brings you to my neck of the woods?" she asked. Before Gina could speak, Dahlia introduced herself to the strange woman. "Hi, my name is Dahlia."

The unidentified woman spoke back. "Hi, my name is Kim." Dahlia noticed the heavy Jamaican accent right away. Aside from the woman's accent, there was something familiar about her, Dahlia just couldn't put her finger on it.

"Do I know you?" Dahlia asked.

"No, I'm not from here," Kim answered.

"Well nice to meet you, Kim." Dahlia turned her attention back to Gina. "So, tell me…what brings you to this side of town?"

Before Gina could respond, Kim spoke up.

"I wanted to come over and meet with you." This took Dahlia, and from the look on Gina's face, Gina by surprise. Unlike Rodney and Gina that have been here for a while, her accent seemed as if she hadn't been in America long. The more Kim talked Dahlia felt as if she'd heard her voice before.

"Oh yeah?" Dahlia asked as she glanced at Gina, then returned her focus toward Kim. "How can I help you?"

"First, you can start off by letting me know how serious you and Rodney are," Kim said.

Dahlia immediately felt bad vibes. "I don't feel comfortable talking about my relationship, why do you ask?"

"Because he is telling me something and I wanted to hear what you had to say," Kim answered. Dahlia was in disbelief at what the girl asked her, and at the fact that Gina had the audacity to bring drama to her home. Gina didn't even know if her son was there or not. As far as Dahlia was concerned, it was time for them to leave.

"Whatever he told you, is probably what it is," Dahlia said then looked at Gina. "...I see who you are." Dahlia got up and walked toward the door, gesturing for them to follow her. Gina showed no emotions. They got up and followed Dahlia to the door.

"I'll tell Smoke and Mecca that you said hi," Kim said as she slammed the door behind her. It's hard to get under Dahlia's skin, but Kim mentioning her son and his father made her mad as hell. It was bad enough she came asking about Rodney. *"Damn, she knows Smoke and Mecca too?"* she questioned to herself. *"I know damn well this bitch didn't just say that shit to me."* Dahlia reopened the door as fast as she could. "Fuck you, bitch!" she yelled at Kim as loud as she could. "If I find out that you're anywhere near my son, I promise you Imma whoop your ass." Dahlia slammed the door. She couldn't calm herself down as she thought about what just happened.

Dahlia immediately picked up the phone and called Roro. She didn't like telling Roro things like this, but Roro was one of the few people that knew how to calm her down. She dialed Roro's number, almost deciding against telling her before she answered. When Roro finally came to the phone Dahlia was even more upset and filled her in to what just happened.

"Hold up," Roro said as she tried to make sure that what she heard was accurate. Roro was infuriated. "I'm on my way." She hung up in Dahlia's ear.

Roro arrived at Dahlia's house in minutes, wearing a sweatsuit and tennis shoes. "Come on let's go," she said as soon as she walked in.

Dahlia knew what this meant. *"Damn I shouldn't have told her,"* she thought as she grabbed her tennis shoes. She knew how Roro's temper was, but she needed her friend to be a listening ear, not go gangster. She felt like what happened was enough, and now she knew who Gina really was. Her and Gina didn't have to never speak again, that was enough for her. But now they were on their way to do drive-by's and beatdowns.

"I told you that bitch was iffy," Roro said as she paced the floor. "Why didn't you call me while they were here?"

"Everything happened so fast." Dahlia explained. "As soon as the questions started, I immediately shut it down."

"Okay." Roro turned around and opened the door. "I'm outside in the car."

"The car?" Dahlia repeated, coming to the realization that they were going to do some dirt with Mrs. Pat's car. *"Roro isn't thinking"* she thought as she tied her shoestrings.

When she walked outside, Roro was sitting inside the car. Dahlia walked to the driver's side, forcing Roro to roll her window down. "You're going to drive Mrs. Pat's car to do this shit?" she asked, hoping that by her saying that, it would make Roro think more clear.

"Oh bitch, your scared?" Roro asked. "If so, let me know and I can put you on my punk bitch list."

Dahlia assured Roro that she wasn't afraid, but she didn't feel comfortable using Mrs. Pat's car in this situation. "What if Mrs. Pat is driving down the street, not knowing anything, and one of them bitches see her car?"

Dahlia could see the anger in Roro's face as she began to picture that scenario, "...and I would kill every one of them bitches," she answered. "All of them hoes, one by one. That shit would be calculated, and very ugly."

"Yeah, I feel you, but what about Mrs. Pat?" Dahlia questioned.

Roro looked at Dahlia with a straight faced and silent.

"Okay, you got it. I think your ass is scared for real, but Imma let you have it today, being that you wanna bring my momma up in it and shit. But we are going to run into them bitches and it's going to be soon, real soon. I know this because them bitches was brave enough to come to your house with some bullshit. That tells me, that they sense some kind of weakness. You're going to have to drop that fear shit. Those motherfuckers invaded your space. Your son lives here. Bitch you gotta stand for something. If not for yourself, then at least do it for him."

Dahlia knew what she was saying was right. What if Mecca was home? She knew that she was going to have to handle that situation, and do it quickly, because she didn't know when Smoke was bringing him back home. After Roro felt like she said everything that she needed, she told Dahlia that she was going back home, but if they come back, or called her, that she'd better call her. Dahlia agreed, and Roro left. *"This is some messy shit,"* Dahlia mumbled as she watched Mrs. Pat's car drive away down the street.

When Dahlia turned around to walk into the house, she saw her nosey ass neighbor trying to suck up as much information as he could.

"Are you okay baby girl?" he asked, praying that Dahlia would give him any ounce of information to gossip about.

"Yeah, I'm good," she replied as she walked past him and into the house. Dahlia thought about everything Roro said to her and began to question herself. *"Am I really scared?"* She thought back to all the times that Roro got into fights, and how she was never there. Then thought about how every time she got into anything, Roro was always there.

She kept replaying what Roro had asked her. What would have happened if Mecca was home? And how can they have felt comfortable enough to come to her house unannounced. Not only unannounced, but with straight drama. Dahlia noticed how that never happened to Roro because she was known to be crazy. She kept replaying it over and over in her head until she came to the conclusion that she couldn't be nice anymore.

She had to fight one of them hoes, and it was gonna be for a good cause too. They infiltrated her home, and she wasn't cool with that at all. Now the world was going to get a different side of her, and she didn't care how anyone felt. This was what they wanted, so this is what they were gonna get. Whenever she saw them, she planned to fire off, on site. As Dahlia hyped herself up into this overnight gangster, she couldn't help but wonder, "Who am I beginning to turn into?"

CHAPTER 7

A Category One

Dahlia and Roro stood in the line of the juvenile clerks at the courthouse. Dahlia hadn't heard or seen Mecca since he left with Smoke. She tried to call but Smoke wouldn't answer nor return any of her calls. When Dahlia was finally able to speak with a clerk, she explained how she wanted to get custody of her son. Dahlia gave the clerk all of the information she needed as she typed it in the computer.

"Oh," the clerk said and stopped typing.

"What happened?" Dahlia asked as she watched the face of the confused clerk.

"I'll be right back," the clerk said as she walked away from the computer.

"Damn, what's that about?" Roro asked trying to understand what was going on.

"I don't know," Dahlia responded as she leaned on the counter and put her hands on her forehead.

After leaving Dahlia standing at the counter for a while, the clerk finally came back with a paper in her hand. "Ma'am, your son's father already filed for custody of your son," she said as she handed Dahlia the letter.

"What?" Dahlia yelled as she snatched the paper from the clerk's hand. Tears ran down Dahlia's face. "How can he do that...he barely even saw him?" Dahlia questioned.

"I understand your frustration," the clerk said as she grabbed the tissue box handing it to Dahlia. Dahlia took a few tissues from the box and patted her face dry and began to read the letter. Roro put her arm around Dalia's shoulder. "Let's go, he won't have him for long," Roro promised, and they both walked away.

Dahlia cried the whole ride home. "You're coming to my house," Roro demanded. "There is no way you're going home like this."

Dahlia just wanted to go home, get underneath her covers and cry, but she didn't have the strength to fight about it. Every time she tried, her heart would beat harder and the tears would fall faster. When they walked inside Roro's house, Mrs. Pat was in the living room watering her plants. She turned around and asked, "How did things go?" That's when she noticed Dahlia was crying. "What's wrong?" she asked as she walked over to her as fast as she could. She put her arms around Dahlia and hugged her. The warm feeling and comfort that Dahlia felt from Mrs. Pat caused her to cry even more. She cried like a baby, while Roro explained to her mother what happened.

Mrs. Pat put one hand on Dahlia's forehead and the other hand on her stomach and began to pray. Roro came behind Dahlia and put both of her hands on Dahlia's shoulders. Dahlia felt something that she never felt before. Mrs. Pat always prayed for her, but she never felt this before. She began to cry harder, it was an uncontrollable cry, and her mind began to become lighter. Dahlia cried until she couldn't cry any more. She just stood there motionless, with dried up tears on her face while Mrs. Pat continued to pray.

When Mrs. Pat finished praying, she assured Dahlia that God had everything under control. She told her that God loved her, and even in the toughest situations God is always the one holding her up. "Have faith child, he'll never forsake you. You just got to have faith. I'm getting ready to call my prayer warriors, and we're going to get on top of this right away." She gave Dahlia another hug, this one tighter than the last. She then walked to her room and called her friends, so they could continue praying.

That night while Dahlia laid in the bed all she could do was think about Mecca. Dahlia knew that her son asked about her. She wondered What Smoke told him about her. Dahlia couldn't eat earlier that day, and it was obvious that she wasn't going to be able to sleep. She sat up on Jeremiah's bed and glanced over at Roro and Jeremiah peacefully sleeping on Roro's bed. Dahlia didn't want her friend to ever experience what she was going through, but she couldn't help but wish that her son was laying beside her, so she could cuddle with him like she always did when they fell asleep. She began to cry, but this time, she didn't feel the wetness of the tears rolling down her face. She continued to cry as soft as she could.

When Dahlia finally opened her eyes, she glanced over towards her friend's bed and noticed that Roro and Jeremiah were gone. She just laid there, staring at the ceiling. *"I don't want to move,"* she thought to herself. *"I just want to lay here. I don't want to talk. I don't want to walk or comb my hair. I just want my son back."* She began to cry again. She closed her eyes and thought about the last time she saw him. She giggled a little when a picture came to her mind of him lying in the bed with his feet hanging out. She missed her baby.

Dahlia could hear someone walking towards the room; she closed her eyes so they would think that she was still sleep.

"I know that you're not sleeping," Mrs. Pat said. "You have to get up honey....You can't lay here and not live." Mrs. Pat opened the blinds. Dahlia put her arm over her face to cover her eyes from the sun.

"What are you going to do? Just lay here?" Mrs. Pat asked. Dahlia didn't answer. "Well, I'm not going to let you." She walked to the bed and sat beside Dahlia.

"I've seen you go through many things with your baby. Both while his father was and wasn't around. You're a good mother, and trust me, no judge in their right mind is going to take him away from you. Where is your faith child?" she asked. "You've been around me since you were knee high, I know it's in you, now get up. We're going to fight with you, you're not alone, but you have to get up."

While Mrs. Pat talked to Dahlia, they heard a knock on the bedroom door. "Come in," Mrs. Pat said. Dahlia heard someone call her name.

"Mommy!" Dahlia yelled as her mother rushed over to embrace her daughter. "Momma he took him. He took him, Momma," Dahlia cried as she laid her head on her mother's chest.

"I know baby," her mother said as she rubbed Dahlia's hair. "But not for long. Get up. We're going to your house, so you can get dressed. Your dad is in the car waiting, we have somewhere to go." Dahlia got up as her mother and Mrs. Pat requested.

"Let me know when or if you may need me," Mrs. Pat told Dahlia's mother.

"I will," Mrs. Dot replied as they hugged each other. When Dahlia reached the living room, Roro was standing there with tears in her eyes, waiting on Dahlia to walk past. When Dahlia got close enough, she grabbed and hugged her, and they both cried.

"I love you," they repeatedly told each other.

"Okay," Mrs. Pat said. "Y'all can talk later, they have somewhere to be."

They released each other, and Dahlia and her mother left. Dahlia's father didn't have anything to say, and she understood why. Him and Mecca were very close, and he never showed his emotions. In her twenty years, Dahlia had never seen him cry. It was eerily quiet in the car, but Dahlia was alright with that. She didn't have any strength for words, and in actuality, she couldn't even understand how she was even walking.

When they pulled up, Dahlia noticed her nosey next door neighbor sitting on his porch. Dahlia and her mother got out the car and walked toward Dahlia's door.

"Hey baby girl," he said smiling. Dahlia just kept walking. "Hey baby girl," he said again. Dahlia didn't respond as she focused on opening her door. Dahlia's mom took the key from her and unlocked the door. "I'm not going to keep speaking to you," he told Dahlia, irritated that she didn't speak back.

Dahlia's mother opened Dahlia's door. She told her to go ahead and get dressed, and that her and her father would be waiting outside in the car. Dahlia went in the house but could hear her mother fussing and cussing. As she walked past the window, she could see her mother holding her key toward the man, telling him that she'd carve his big eyes out with just the key alone. Dahlia chuckled as she pictured her mother cutting his eyes out with a key. *"Only my mom,"* she thought as she went to the room to get dressed.

When Dahlia walked out of the house, she noticed her neighbor was nowhere in sight. She got into her father's car. Dahlia didn't know where they were going, but she had an idea. She knew how close her parents were with Mecca, and that they would do everything in their power to get him back. She didn't want to ask or carry on any type of conversation, so whatever she had to do or wherever she had to go, she was all for it—as long as Mecca was on his way home.

They parked in front of what looked like office buildings. When they went inside, she knew exactly what it was about. They were going to speak with a lawyer. Dahlia felt an overwhelming indescribable feeling; she was blessed to have parents that would go the distance with her, going out of their way to put in the money and resources to help her when difficult situations would arise. She thought of all the young women who didn't have that. Women who had no one, and just had to pray that nothing like what she was going through would happen to them because the outcome would probably be much worse.

Dahlia and her parents sat in the waiting area briefly before the assistant called them back to meet with the lawyer. Dahlia followed her parents as they walked into the lawyers office and sat at the long round table. Dahlia and her father listened as her mother told the lawyer everything she knew about the situation.

"What else do I need to know?" the lawyer asked as he turned toward Dahlia.

She looked back at him, "Do you think that you could help us?...I mean if you had to go on only what my mother said, could you help us?" Dahlia asked.

The lawyer sat back in his chair and looked in Dahlia's eyes. "I think I can do a lot of good with what your mother has already told me. But if you have any more information to help me, I'm more than sure I can get your son back."

Dahlia told him everything that she could think of that she felt would help in any way to get her baby boy back.

At the end of the meeting, the lawyer shook their hands, and assured them that he would be in contact very soon. Dahlia left feeling better than what she felt when she came in. The hurt was still there, but she could now see a light at the end of the tunnel. She was even able to eat a little when they stopped at a local fast food restaurant. It was only a small fry, but considering she couldn't eat at all, it was a start.

Dahlia's parents tried to get her to stay with them, but she refused. She just wanted to spend some time alone and reflect on the situation. She wanted to lay in her bed, and cry, yell out loud, all of that. Even though her parents wouldn't judge her because of her feelings, she preferred to go through it alone.

"Okay," her mother said, "but if you have any issues, call me. And if your neighbor so much as blinks in your direction, call me ASAP."

Dahlia's father looked at his wife and shook his head. "I love you," he told Dahlia. "I'm here if you need me, you know that right?"

"Yeah, I know Daddy," she answered as she got out of the car. Dahlia's parents waited until she went in the house, and then they drove off.

Dahlia laid in the bed for the next two days, only to get up to use the restroom. With the way she was feeling, if the toilet could come to her room, she wouldn't get up for that either. She didn't go to work, take a shower, brush her teeth...nothing. She just laid there thinking about Mecca. She talked to Roro, Mrs. Pat and her parents, but still no sign of Mecca. *"How could he do this to me?"* she thought. She felt as though Smoke was going out of his way to hurt her, and she couldn't understand it. *"I never would have done this to him."* Tears ran down her face. Dahlia thought about all of the times when she put Smoke's needs before her own. Times when it was just her and Mecca struggling, eating noodles alone and he was nowhere in sight.

As Dahlia was in deep thought, the phone rang. She jumped up and ran into the living room to answer it, hoping it was Mecca.

"Hello," she answered, picking up the phone as fast as she could. Instead, she heard "You have a free call from 'Red'." Her heart began to pump extra hard. Now, she could finally get to the bottom of how he knew Smoke and what happened to make him feel the need to take their son.

"Hello?" Rodney questioned, realizing she had accepted his call.

"Hello," Dahlia responded and immediately went in with her questioning. "How do you know Smoke?"

Before he could answer, she followed with another, "...And why didn't you tell me that you knew him?"

"...He's dating my ex, that's how I met him," Rodney explained.

"Your ex?" Dahlia asked surprised. "Who, Kim?"

"Yeah," he answered, sounding confused. "How do you know Kim?"

Dahlia explained everything that's been going on, from Gina bringing Kim to her house to Smoke taking Mecca. Rodney explained that he had already met Mecca a few times previously when he was with Kim.

"What?" she yelled. "You knew my son and held all of that back from me? So what, me and Mecca are in the middle of some type of game that y'all have going on? I didn't even know that I was playing a game, let alone with my son." She couldn't believe what she heard. "You played with me to get to him?" she questioned, but felt she already knew the answer.

Rodney told Dahlia that it wasn't like that, but she didn't want to hear it. He gave her all the information she needed, and as far as she was concerned, they had nothing else to talk about. Dahlia never wanted to see him, nor hear his voice again and she wanted to make sure he understood that. "Never call my phone again," she yelled and slammed her phone down as hard as she could without breaking it.

Dahlia wasn't upset anymore, at this point she was in a furious rage. The phone rang over and over, but Dahlia didn't answer it. She knew who it was, and they had nothing else to talk about. This was the last game that she would play with anyone, in any type of relationship, whether platonic or romantic. It is said that whenever we go through any kind of hurt or realization in a relationship, we hold on to different aspects of it, either good or bad. She took something that she would carry with her for the rest of her life. And at that moment, she didn't understand it; she just knew that she was beginning to feel different. A new Dahlia was being born, and she was happy about it.

CHAPTER 8

A Category Two

Dahlia and Roro had begun going out on a regular basis now. Roro thought that one of the ways to keep Dahlia's mind off of all of the drama surrounding her life, was to get her out of the house and into the night life, Dahlia hesitantly agreed. As far as they were concerned, anything beat sitting in the house waiting on a phone call, that may or may not come. Dahlia needed a different scene, instead of the surrounding walls that she stared at day in and day out.

One night they decided not to go to the club; they opted for a local bar instead. They went inside and sat at the bar, examining the room as they usually did to see who was inside. As they sipped their drinks, they noticed a crowd forming. In the middle of the chaos, they noticed two women. The tension seemed to escalate, not from the women themselves, instead from the people around them fueling them. It was as if they both had something to prove to the crowd. Before they knew it, the tension between the two ladies was beyond control and a full fledge fight was in progress. Dahlia and Roro giggled as they watched the two women grabbing each other's hair extensions.

"That's the first thing we go for," Dahlia said to Roro. The two women fell on the floor, they both still had hair in each palm. Roro looked at the women like a comedy; she expected more punches to be thrown.

"Naw," she told Dahlia, "that's what your non-fighting ass go for... I'm going for something else. Fuck all that pulling hair shit, the hair ain't do shit to me. I want your body to feel it, and your mind to always remember who I am. Let me find out that you're a hair extension collector." She paused and looked at Dahlia with compassion, "If you're in need of hair extensions, I have a whole drawer full at the house."

"Fuck you," Dahlia responded and took a sip from her drink.

"Naw, seriously," Roro continued. "It's 100% human. You don't have to go through these lonely souls to collect used and abused hairs." They both laughed hysterically.

"Your ass is crazy," Dahlia said as they watched the bouncers pull the women apart.

From out of nowhere a shoe flew across the room and hit Dahlia directly in her nose. Dahlia grabbed her nose; her and Roro both stood up, immediately looking into the direction that the flying shoe came from. Kim, Gina , and a few other females were standing on the opposite side of the room, talking and watching them.

"Who threw the fucking shoe?" Dahlia yelled across the room as she charged toward them. None of the women said anything. They watched her in silence. "Which one of you bitches threw the fucking shoe at me while I wasn't looking? Whoever did it is a pure BITCH!" She paused to allow them to speak, but they were still quiet.

She continued, "That's some straight bitch shit! I'm facing y'all, do that shit now!"

By this time Roro was standing slightly in front of Dahlia. Roro noticed a beer bottle sitting on the table and grabbed it. She never said anything, just kept walking forward, sizing up all of the women. She mostly kept her eyes on Gina though. By the way she was looking at Gina, Gina knew if anything erupted, she would be the first person that Roro would go after. Roro launched the bottle toward Gina, not caring who it hit. The women were surprised that Roro actually threw the bottle at them as they barely ducked out of the way of the flying glass. The bouncers heard the bottle scatter as it hit the ground. Some of the security team left the other two women and ran towards Dahlia and Roro.

This time it was Dahlia that was in need of being calmed by security. She wanted someone to pay for hitting her, but more for being comfortable thinking they could get away with it. She had a lot on her mind, and part of her problems stemmed from the same bitches that stood directly in front of her. Dahlia constantly tried to think of ways to get around to the group of women. The more she thought about Kim, and all of the things that Rodney exposed to her, she wanted blood. Dahlia began to think of Kim holding Mecca at night, fixing him breakfast, lunch, and dinner, which made her even angrier.

Then those thoughts began to change. The feelings Dahlia had of Kim doing all of the things that she couldn't do, changed into Kim doing things to Mecca that she wouldn't do. Dahlia did something that she never in a million years, thought that she would. She fought with bouncers to get to Kim. The whole time she was fighting them, she had her eyes on Kim. She had tunnel vision, and she wanted blood.

The next thing Dahlia knew, she and Roro were standing outside of the bar after being put out. Dahlia and Roro were told to leave the premises or the police would be called. Dahlia and Roro left the premises, only to park around the corner. They stayed there and waited for Kim and her groupies to leave. After a couple of hours of waiting, they saw Smoke's car leaving the parking lot. Roro followed Smoke's car, trying not to be noticed.

"These bitches are driving past your house," Roro said and sped up. Dahlia's heart was pumping harder than ever before. She needed some action.

Kim looked in her review mirror and noticed Roro and Dahlia following them, so she pulled over. Roro grabbed her bumper jack, from under the driver's seat while Dahlia grabbed the box cutter from out of the glove compartment. Once Roro and Dahlia jumped out of the car, running towards Smoke's car, Kim took off. She made a U-turn in the middle of the street and went out of her way attempting to hit them with Smoke's car. Roro threw the bumper jack at the car and shattered the back window as the car sped off.

"Do you know where they live?" Roro asked as her and Dahlia ran to the car as fast as they could, trying to catch up with them.

"Damn," Dahlia yelled, hitting Mrs. Pat's dashboard. "He never told me where he lived."

They drove around as long as they could trying to find Smoke and Kim's house, but came up empty-handed. "There's always another day," Roro said as she started driving home. She briefly turned to Dahlia in amazement, "Look at you, Mrs. I'm gonna kick yo ass! What the fuck happened to you bitch?" She was excited for the changes that her best friend was showing.

"I'm tired of these bitches," Dahlia said and sunk down in the passenger seat. "I don't fuck with nobody, why fuck with me?"

Roro listened to Dahlia as she vented. "You mean you really don't see it? Come on now. It's obvious that jealousy is playing a part. They come to your house...throw a shoe. They do everything in their power to disrupt your life, right?" Roro asked. "Why would any person do that if they didn't feel threatened?" Dahlia shook her head in agreement.

"I just can't see no one putting so much energy in someone or something that they had no type of feelings towards," Roro continued, "whether the feelings were good or bad. I mean, if she's already with Smoke, why fuck with you? She already got the goods, right?"

"Right," Dahlia confirmed, still angry.

After Roro dropped Dahlia off, Dahlia jumped in the shower, jumped in her bed, and cuddled under her blanket. She began to doze off, when she heard her phone ringing. She jumped up and ran into the living room to answer it. Before she could say hello, Smoke was on the other end of the phone, yelling fussing and cursing her out about his car window.

"Bitch you ain't like that for real," he yelled. He yelled everything he could to berate her. To make her feel less than like he would usually do right before they broke up.

Dahlia had a long night and just wanted peace. More than that, she wanted her baby back, so she tried her best not to upset him more than he already was. "Well, did she tell you that she tried to hit us with your car?"

It was as though Smoke didn't hear anything by the way he went straight into calling her a nothing ass bitch and told her how she would never have anything or anyone to love her.

Dahlia became frustrated. Not only from the ugly names he was calling her, but by the fact that she couldn't get a word in, and the one thing that she did say, involved her life and he simply didn't give a damn. Them having a conversation, to her was purposeless. The only way to get Mecca back was to get straight to the point. Fuck all of this shit. She wasn't the same person that she was when he last seen her. He changed her, in a way that she didn't yet understand.

"Look," Dahlia said, in a stern tone, "where is Mecca?"

"He's with his real momma," he said without hesitation. Those words shook Dahlia's soul. But she had to try everything in her power to get her son back, keeping calm was the key.

"Real mother?" she asked. "No honey, the only mother Mecca has is me. And you nor your dumb ass bitch can ever change that."

"Okay, so how would you feel if I told you that Rodney was going to be his real daddy...did she tell you that she came to my house asking about me and Rodney?"

No matter how much Dahlia tried to hide her emotions, Rodney could still sense her fear. And that fear was losing Mecca. He knew that Mecca meant the world to her, so he had to cut her. "I promise you," he said through gritted teeth. "You'll never see me and Kim's son again, I can bet my life on it." He hung the phone up in her ear.

She held the phone with the dial tone beeping in her ear. She knew Smoke very well. And whenever he promised something, that's what he meant. She thought about her parents getting her the lawyer. She was thankful that she didn't let her anger give away the surprise that he was going to feel once he entered the courtroom. He wouldn't except that coming from his salary. And if he had any knowledge of that, he would most definitely lawyer up. For that reason alone, she felt like she dodged a bullet. She became even happier as she pictured the look his face once the judge would reveal that her, "a no good for nothing ass bitch", is awarded full custody of his son. *"We'll see who gets the last laugh,"* she said, finally hanging up the phone.

CHAPTER 9

A Category Three

D ahlia's parents blew the horn excessively, rushing her to come out of the house. Any other time Dahlia would be irritated, but today, her parents had good reason to rush her. The day had finally arrived for court, and they all would be happy, leaving the courthouse with Mecca. She had planned all the things that they would do once he came home. Hide and seek, look at the stars, and find something new other than the Big Dipper. She even brought the chocolate chip cookies that he liked to help her bake. While the next day, her and Roro had planned something fun with the boys. They were going to have so much fun. She was excited, and couldn't wait to see, feel and kiss her baby again.

When they entered the courtroom, they seen Smoke and Kim, but noticed that they didn't have Mecca.

"Where is Mecca?" Mrs. Dot asked.

"I don't know Mom, maybe Smoke didn't want him to witness all of the drama," Dahlia responded, trying to make sense of it.

"You mean the drama that he created?" Mrs. Dot asked. Dahlia laughed; her mother was always straight to the point.

"Yeah Mom, that drama."

When they were called to go up, everything Dahlia expected to happen, happened. Not that Smoke didn't put up a fight. He talked about how Dahlia couldn't afford to take care of their son, how she lived in a terrible neighborhood, and even tried lying under oath, that she kept Mecca from him. Although what he said made Dahlia angry, she didn't respond, just as her lawyer informed. She kept quiet until the judge spoke to her. Smoke on the other hand kept interrupting her while she spoke; he even talked over the judge while the judge tried to get him to wait his turn to speak. At one point, he even went back and forth with the judge. That all played right in their favor. In the end, Dahlia was awarded full custody of Mecca, with visitation to Smoke. And because Smoke had talked about how Dahlia struggled with their son, Smoke was also forced to pay child support.

Smoke turned to Dahlia while the judge spoke. He had a look on his face that Dahlia, even knowing him so long, had never seen before. His veins popped out of his forehead and neck... *"Nope, I'll kill you first,"* he mouthed his lips, making sure that she was the only one who could see it. Dahlia felt a little fear from what he said to and the look he gave her, but the overwhelming joy she felt about getting Mecca back home where he belonged took over any fear that he could give her. She got what she wanted and needed, plus some with the extra money granted to help her take care of her son.

Unlike Dahlia, her father didn't appreciate the way Smoke stared at his daughter. "Is there a problem?" her father blurted out. Smoke looked at Dahlia's father with the same expression that he did Dahlia then turned towards the judge and smiled. He never looked in their direction again.

"No, there isn't a problem."

Because Mecca wasn't at the courthouse, the judge ordered Smoke to meet Dahlia at the precinct to hand over his son to Dahlia no later than 3:00 that day. Smoke agreed, and they all left. Dahlia was the happiest she'd been since she gave birth to Mecca.

By the time they got out of the courtroom, it was already 1:00. So, they decided to waste some time until 3:00. They stopped at Golden Coral and sat down to eat. Dahlia ate and ate, more than she had been able to eat in a long time. She had started to feel like herself again. She didn't even feel as much anger towards Kim; she still wanted to whip her ass, just not as bad now.

After Golden Coral, they stopped by the mall. Mrs. Dot had to pick Mecca an outfit to take family pictures in, which she had just decided without Dahlia or her father's consent. They didn't mind though. They all understood the happiness that each of them felt, and it was all that mattered—the happiness from Mecca's return. Once they wrapped things up at the mall, they headed to the precinct. They arrived fifteen minutes early and decided to go inside and wait.

An hour and a half later, Dahlia was nervous. She remembered how upset he was in the courtroom, and him telling her he wasn't giving Mecca back. Dahlia and her parents went to the nearest payphone, and she called him. She didn't understand why he would be late for what the judge had ordered him to do. Smoke had been in front of a judge, plenty of times, and he never went against what the judge said. Not that he feared jail, he just always felt like he could do more on the streets than he could locked up.

Smoke answered the phone, surprised to hear Dahlia. "Whose phone number is this?" he asked immediately.

"Where are you?" she asked. "You were supposed to have been here almost two hours ago. Smoke ignored Dahlia's question. She didn't want to go back and forth, she just wanted Mecca. She decided to go ahead and tell him that she was at a pay phone.

"You're near the precinct?" he asked as if he didn't hear what she had just told him.

"Yes." She sighed but was happy that he finally seemed to be on the same page.

"I'll be there." He hung up in her ear. He never told Dahlia when he was coming, so she immediately called him back, but this time he didn't answer.

Dahlia and her parents sat in the precinct until 7:00 that night attempting to reach Smoke again several times throughout; he didn't show or answer. Dahlia knew more than ever now that he was going to stay true to his words. When he promised her that she would never see Mecca again, that's what he meant.

Dahlia got back in the car with her parents and explained to them that she didn't think Smoke was bringing Mecca, and that they might as well go home.

"He's so stupid," she said to her parents on the drive home.

"They know where he lives. They have his address at the courthouse. It's okay," Mrs. Dot said. "We'll be right back at the courthouse tomorrow. Oh, he's giving up my boy." Tears filled her mother's eyes, and her voice cracked.

"Ma, he's not that stupid," Dahlia said, trying to stop her mother from crying before she started.

"I know," she said as she wiped her eyes.

Once Dahlia got inside the house, she called Smoke back to back. He still didn't answer his phone. *"How did I stay with him so long?"* she asked herself, irritated that he had her and her parents sitting in the precinct so long. "I hope they lock his dumb ass up," she said to herself aloud. "Fucking asshole!"

The next day, Dahlia waited for her parents to come to get her again. She sat by the window so that she could dash out the door as soon as they arrived. She didn't want to play with Smoke anymore, he was doing entirely too much. And to her, it all felt personal. She couldn't understand though because he was the one that cheated and left her. She had never done anything to harm him. She even went out of her way to put her life on hold, just to satisfy him.

Her parents arrived and before Dahlia could open the door, they were already knocking. When Dahlia opened the door her mother and father walked inside. They began explaining how they didn't have to go back to the courthouse, they only had to call the police and let them handle it. It was out of their hands now. Dahlia called the police to fill them in on what happened, they took her information and told her someone would be in contact shortly. She waited on a call back so they could know when and where they could pick Mecca up.

Mrs. Dot answered the phone when the police finally called them back three hours later. Dahlia watched her mom scream as she fell to the floor crying. Dahlia's heart stopped beating. Her legs became numb as she rushed to the phone. Dahlia picked the phone up, afraid to hear the same thing that her mother heard but knowing she had to. Dahlia's father consoled his wife while Dahlia talked to the officer.

"Hello," Dahlia said.

"Hello, is this Mrs. Dahlia Sutherland?" he asked.

"Yes, it is."

"Ma'am, this is officer Tatum. We have reason to believe that your son's father Jordan Stein left the country with your son this morning."

"No," Dahlia responded, not wanting to believe what the officer was saying.

"They moved to Jamaica, ma'am."

"No," Dahlia repeated over and over. "How could he do that?... I mean, can he get away with this?"

"We're going to do everything in our power to return your son home to you," Officer Tatum said. "We're in the process of contacting the Jamaican authorities now."

Dahlia thanked him and slowly hung up the phone. "He took my son," she repeated over and over again. Each time she repeated it, the louder she became, until she was screaming it at the top of her lungs. Her father was in disbelief. But at the same time, he did the only thing he could do at that time—consoled his wife and his daughter.

After Dahlia's parents left, she constantly called Smoke's phone, praying that the police were misinformed. However, it was the same outcome each time. Reality sank in. Her son was in a whole different country, and she couldn't do anything about it but wait on some police officers to hopefully save him. Dahlia laid in the bed that night and cried a tearless cry until she finally drifted off to sleep.

The next day Dahlia was awakened by the loud sound of banging on her door. She didn't want to answer it but felt it may be something important. And besides, it could have been the police with good news about Mecca. With that thought, she rushed to the door. When she opened it, she saw Roro standing there with a pillow, a blanket, and an overnight bag. Roro walked inside, laid her things on the couch and hugged her friend. They both cried together.

"I got you," Roro kept repeating to her friend. "I promise you. This is our battle, not just yours."

Dahlia felt a tear finally fall. But without any other tears following. She knew her friend had her back without a question, and the feeling was mutual.

"I called the job," Roro said. "You're off for a couple of weeks."

Dahlia opened her eyes as wide as she could. "You told them about Mecca?"

Roro looked at Dahlia with that look that she sometimes gave people. It was a look of "come on now, do you think I'm that dumb?" Any other time she would start the sentence off with bitch, but not today. "I told them you had family issues that you had to work out and left it at that...by the way did you eat anything?" Roro asked.

"Thanks Roro," Dahlia said, "but why aren't you at work? And yes, I did already eat."

"I'm off because we have the same family, and you're lying about eating," Roro said. "I'm going to tell you how I know. You just talked to me with that same funky ass breath from yesterday, which means you still haven't brushed your teeth yet…nor showered. The crust around your eyes is giving that away. Not to mention, I knocked on your door for a while, so you had to have just gotten up. Dahlia smiled at her friend, but something inside kept her from laughing. "Go ahead and take your shower, Imma fix you something to eat."

Dahlia looked at Roro ready to protest but before she could, Roro told her that she had to eat and that she was going to make sure of it, even if she had to shove the food down her throat herself.

"Now I would hate to have to do that, being that I love you and all, but at the end of the day…I love Mecca more. He needs you to be strong enough mentally and physically to fight for him, and you need food to do that.

So, chop, chop...now carry on and wash your ass," Roro said.

Dahlia turned and walked toward the bathroom to take a shower. As Dahlia opened up the bathroom door, Roro yelled down the hallway, "And whatever you do, please get some toothpaste and mouthwash circulating, thank you."

Dahlia let out a little chuckle, as she walked into her restroom, hearing her friend still mumbling about her breath. "That shit don't make no sense, and I literally mean shit," she heard Roro say. Dahlia held her hand up to cover her nose and blew her breath into her hand. "Dang," she said and laughed silently.

As Dahlia stood in the hot shower, the warm water felt extremely comfortable running over her body. The water felt rejuvenating and like it somehow cleansed her soul. It was short lived before Mecca drifted back into her mind. She wondered what he was doing, and how Kim was treating him. He was with Smoke, yeah, and she knew Smoke would never let anything happen to him.

But they were in Kim's world now and Dahlia knew nothing about her. Everything she knew about her so far wasn't good, and sometimes people have the tendency to take things out on kids, that they really want to take out on their parents.

After Dahlia got dressed, she ate as much of the breakfast that she could because she knew deep inside, what Roro was saying was correct. She had to keep her strength, but her stomach wasn't agreeing with her. All of her emotions were going back and forth from her heart to her stomach, and her love for people and food were diminishing. She loved Smoke and look at how he treated her. She loved Mecca and he was taken away from her. She was starting to love Rodney, and he was now in jail for murder, and to her it seemed to be part of the reason that Smoke took Mecca.

Roro and Dahlia talked about everything Dahlia was going through. Roro listened mostly but made small jokes here and there when she sensed Dahlia beginning to feel sad. "Well, I can tell you this," Roro began, "If

Smoke feels Kim, Slim or whatever her fucking name is, doing anything to Mecca he's going to snap. Get that one thing out of your mind. That's exactly where it is, in your mind. That shit ain't going to happen, and deep down inside, you know it ain't."

Dahlia agreed. Smoke loved Mecca, so much so that he would leave the country with their son, against the judge's order.

The phone rang and they both looked at each other.

"Are you not going to answer that?" Roro asked, getting up to answer it. "Oh, hey Ma. ...Oh, okay, I'll be there in a few," she said and hung up the phone. Roro turned around and looked at Dahlia.

"Are you okay?" Dahlia assured that she was fine. "Are you sure?"

"Yes, crazy," Dahlia responded, trying to make light of how she was really feeling. "I'm sure."

"Okay, I'll be right back," Roro said and left out the door.

Roro returned as quickly as she left. "I have good news," she said with a bright smile on her face. "Momma called and told me that GOD had put it in her spirit for me to call Jay."

"Jay?" Dahlia asked. What did he say?"

"Yeah, I didn't want to say anything until after I spoke with him. He said that he talked to them, and that Mecca is doing okay. He claimed to have known nothing about court or anything, but of course he would say that. His ugly ass sister is on her way to jail. I wanted to curse his ass out, but I think that momma is on to something because I feel like we're going to need him eventually."

Even though what Roro told her made Dahlia feel a little better, she just wanted to hold Mecca.

"You know that I love you right?" Roro asked hesitantly.

"Yeah, I know...what else is it Roro?"

"Okay," Roro continued hesitantly. "How do you feel about Red?"

"Who, Rodney?" Dahlia asked. "Ummm, I don't know. I don't know what to think about him now."

"If that's the case, I feel better saying it then."

"Spit it out Roro!" Dahlia rushed.

Roro took a deep breath and began to explain what Jay had told her. "When Smoke and Kim started dating, she was married and still is."

"Okay...but what do that have to do with Rodney?"

"Everything," Roro answered. "Because he's her husband."

CHAPTER 10

A Category Four

A year had gone by since Smoke took Mecca. Dahlia still hadn't heard anything from him, which means that she hadn't heard from Mecca. Rodney hadn't called again the entire time either. Roro hadn't kept in contact with Jay, outside of occasionally checking in about Mecca. Dahlia's life had been pretty stagnant for the past year. She still constantly called the detective in charge of her case, only to always receive the same lack of progress.

Dahlia and Roro started going out every weekend and even some days after work, anything to keep her mind in a better space. Sometimes they would just ride around town lurking, to see or find things to do.

This particular day, they decided to stop by Terri's house. When they walked inside, they noticed Terri had a few friends over, and she was already gossiping about everything she knew. Dahlia felt that everyone came to Terri's house just to get the latest news, which Terri always knew.

"Hey girl," Terri said looking at Roro, not acknowledging Dahlia.

"Hey, what's up?" Roro said as her and Dahlia took a seat to listen to the latest news.

"Girl yeah. Tom was the one who shot that girl for real. Toni had nothing to do with that shit! That boy is in jail for some shit that he didn't even do. He even pistol whipped Junior and threatened to get him killed if he says anything. I'm telling y'all, that motherfucker is crazy. I can't see his ass lasting out here in these streets much longer at the rate he's going," Terri gossiped.

Dahlia could sense tension in the air, but she didn't know where or who it was coming from. When Dahlia looked up, she noticed Terri looking at her as if she wanted to say something. "What?" Dahlia asked Terri.

"What do you mean what?" Terri asked in a sarcastic yet confused tone.

"I mean you're staring at me, as if it's something that you want to say, what is it? Just say it."

"Bitch you're in my damn house, I can look whenever and wherever I damn well please."

"Damn," Roro responded. "Where in the hell did that come from?" Roro glanced over at an infuriated Dahlia. Roro hadn't seen that look since that one night at the club, when she was hit in the nose.

"Yeah bitch," Dahlia yelled. "This is your house, but what motherfucker? Do you want me to leave? I didn't want to come over to this dirty motherfucker anyway. Always talking shit, bitch yeah, I'll get out." She paused and looked around the room in disgust. "You're always talking about the next motherfuckers problems, but your ass is probably dirty as hell. It can't be clean bitch because your house ain't."

"Oops, time to go," Roro said as she jumped up and tapped Dahlia on the shoulder, nudging her to walk toward the door.

"Yes leave," Terri said, surprised at Dahlia's outburst. "I hope you get your son back, bitch."

Those words stunned Dahlia and Roro. Dahlia stood there as she felt her hold body tense up and become extremely hot. She could hear Roro whisper in her ear softly, "Whip her ass." Dahlia did exactly that.

Dahlia ran toward Terri, sensing the fear in her eyes, knowing she had fucked up. Terri turned and ran toward the kitchen, and Dahlia knew in her heart that she couldn't let her get there. Knowing what would happen if Terri were to reach the kitchen caused Dahlia to feel as though she had to fight for her life.

Dahlia grabbed Terri by her long weave and yanked Terri's head back, forcing her to fall backward. Before she hit the ground, Dahlia had already begun punching Terri in her face. She kept punching her until she got tired, then she started banging Terri's head on the floor.

One of the young ladies in the house jumped up to pull Dahlia off of Terri but Roro pushed her out of the way.

"Don't put your fucking hands on my sister," Roro screamed at the girl.

"She's going to kill her," one of the other girls yelled.

Roro knew the girl was right and felt she had to intervene. She grabbed Dahlia and the other girl grabbed Terri. When they pulled them apart, Dahlia wouldn't let Terri's weave go just yet. Instead, she guided Terri's face right into her knee, and blood from Terri's nose went everywhere. Now, Dahlia was finished and Roro didn't have to hold her any longer. Dahlia peacefully walked out of the door. Before closing it, she threw a few of Terri's tracks back where they belonged.

As they got in the car, Roro looked Dahlia up and down, seemingly stunned. "Who the fuck are you, and where in the hell is my damn sister?" she asked. Dahlia didn't respond, she just looked at Roro with a smirk on her face. "Seriously, are you possessed?" Roro raised her two index fingers, making a cross.

"Bitch shut up and let's go before that bitch come out here with a damn knife, gun, or something," Dahlia said. Roro looked as if she felt more comfortable.

"Okay, there she goes," Roro said and peeled off.

Dahlia felt relieved. She was finally able to release some of the stress of not seeing Mecca after a year. She turned up the radio. Now she was able to hit the town, feeling a whole lot better.

After they went to a few clubs, they decided to call it a night and Roro dropped Dahlia off. As soon as Dahlia walked in her house, she grabbed a towel and headed toward the bathroom. She looked in the mirror at her face and noticed a few scratches. *"Oh well. It was worth it,"* she thought to herself. After her shower, she hopped in bed and reached for her alarm clock to turn it off. Thank God that she was off the following day. She hadn't been in a fight in years so she didn't know how sore she would feel in the morning.

As she lay in her bed, Dahlia remembered when her grandfather told her that whenever she was in a fight, for any reason, to throw her first punch with all of her strength. Her Uncle added to the conversation when his father went to the restroom. He told her to always be the one to throw the first blow because this would catch the other person off guard.

"When they're prepared for a hit, they'll be ready, and at a fighting stance. But if they aren't ready and you punch them with all of your might," her uncle said and paused to show her the different places to aim for. "They wouldn't have any other choice, but to fall to the ground. Never stop fighting until you are pulled apart," he advised.

She did everything that they both told her to do tonight. *"I hope you're proud of me, Grandad,"* she whispered, looking towards the ceiling. Maybe it was the hot shower or the fight tiring her out. Whatever it was, it hit her out of nowhere and knocked her sound asleep.

Dahlia all of a sudden heard her bedroom door burst open. *"Not again,"* she thought, looking up at the same tall guy as he looked down at her laying in her bed. The guy grabbed Dahlia by her throat and began to choke her. *"This is it,"* she thought as she tried to fight him back. But he was too strong. It was as if nothing she did hurt him. She hit him, bit him, kicked him, hell…she even stabbed him. He didn't feel any pain.

He wanted Dahlia dead for some unknown reason. From out of nowhere, a gun appeared on the bed beside her. She picked it up and put her finger on the trigger. She heard the footsteps of someone running from her kitchen toward her room, then a loud knock on the door. She opened her eyes from her slumber and immediately jumped up and ran toward the door.

When Dahlia opened the door, she saw her nosey next door neighbor standing there with a cup in his hand.

"Do you have any sugar?" he asked.

"Sure, I do," she said. "Come in and wait while I get it for you."

The neighbor didn't know how to take Dahlia's sudden change in attitude. For the last year, she had hardly spoke to him, so this had him confused. He was already afraid to ask her for sugar, but now she was inviting him inside. He curiously tried to look behind her to see if there was someone standing behind her to knock him upside the head before entering. "Uh, yes, I can come in and wait," he said cautiously.

Dahlia took the cup from her neighbor and went into the kitchen. She sat the cup on her counter thinking about the nightmare she just had. *"He saved my life,"* she thought as she grabbed a Food Lion bag and pour sugar in it. If she had more than one bag, she would have given him the entire bag. Once Dahlia returned with his empty cup and bag of sugar, the man was now sure that Dahlia was out to get him. "You have a good day," she told him as she walked him to the door.

"O-Okay," he said stuttering as he walked out.

Dahlia quickly turned the tv on, not quite wanting to go back to sleep yet. This dream was way different than the others because he put his hands on her in this one. She could also hear someone else in the house, running from her kitchen. She had to get her mind off of that dream for now. She made herself a cup of coffee, sat on the couch and flicked through the channels, deciding on The Ricky Lake show, right before Roro called.

"Bitch, what is your Dr. Jekyll and Mrs. Hyde ass doing?" she asked laughing.

"Nothing, watching Ricky Lake."

"Well, your ass need to be up there on that damn show yourself. You have the nerve to call me crazy. You know that you broke that bitch nose last night, right?"

"Oh, yeah?" Dahlia asked.

"...Bitch stop playing. I'm serious, everyone is talking about that shit."

Dahlia and Roro laughed at how everything happened and how the news was now being casted.

"I guess karma is a real bitch," Dahlia said, thinking about all the gossip she had contributed spreading.

"Huh?" Roro asked, making sure that she heard this new Dahlia right.

"I guess it is," Dahlia answered, coming to her own conclusion. Dahlia wasn't happy about breaking Terri's nose but those words still stung, even a day later. "Fuck that bitch," Dahlia said. Roro agreed and they changed the subject.

Later that night, Dahlia found a good movie to watch on as she curled up on the couch where she would be sleeping that night. It made her feel a little safer than her bed for some reason. While watching the movie, the phone rang. She looked at the caller I.D., and when she realized who it was, her heart beat faster. It was Rodney. Dahlia picked the phone up as fast as she could.

"Hello," he said.

"Hello," Dahlia responded.

"What are you doing out there fighting?" he asked. "That ain't even like you."

"What?" she asked. "I haven't talked to you in a year, and that's the best line you could come up with?"

Rodney laughed. "Naw, you know, the last time we talked...I knew you were upset and didn't think you wanted to talk to me anymore."

"How did you find out so fast anyway?" Dahlia asked. "It just happened."

"Jay told me," he answered.

"Jay?" Dahlia asked. "You mean your brother-in-law Jay?"

"What?...Who told you that?" Rodney asked, shocked that she knew.

"Don't worry about it, just know I know."

"Well, your wife and my babydaddy stole my son, and is now living in Jamaica."

Rodney seemed surprised to hear that. "What do you mean stole?"

"I mean stole, as in steal!" Dahlia confirmed. "The judge gave me custody, and they left the country."

"What are you talking about?" he asked, still not understanding what she was saying. "Kim told her brother that Smoke was awarded custody, and they left the country because your dad put a hit out on him."

Dahlia was appalled at what Rodney had just shared; the lies they were telling blew her away.

"My daddy ain't even like that. And if he was, he would've had his ass killed years ago. They stole my baby. That's what happened. I have the paperwork to prove it."

Listening to Dahlia tell the events that led up to them actually going to court left Rodney dumbfounded. "Let me call you back," he said when she finished and quickly hung up the phone.

Dahlia sat by the phone waiting on Rodney to call. An hour later, he finally did. This time, with beneficial information. He gave her Kim's full name, current job and her and Smoke's address. Dahlia could tell that he felt bad about the situation after hearing the truth, and he proved it by going out of his way to give her the much needed information. She still didn't fully trust him, and didn't know if she ever would. Even though speaking with him brought all of the feelings that she had for him back, she couldn't tell if his feelings were genuine.

When she got off the phone with Rodney, Dahlia called the detective and gave him all of the information Rodney gave her.

"Thanks for this," the detective said. "We'll get back in touch with you as soon as we can."

"As soon as you can? Well how soon is that?" she asked, upset with his lack of empathy. She understood that she wasn't the only case that he had, but she didn't understand his tone of voice.

"As soon as we can ma'am, is there anything else?" he asked, sounding irritated.

"No, there isn't," Dahlia responded and hung up in the detective's ear.

"I hope this didn't hinder our case," she thought as she debated on whether or not to call him back. *"Oh well, I'll*

call him back tomorrow. The way he was talking to me on the phone, I don't want to make it worse. Besides, I have to prepare for work tomorrow." Especially after the goldmine that Rodney just gave her. She already wanted to call her parents and call out. But she didn't want to get her parents hopes up high, for something that may not be concrete. They were already going through enough. Dahlia took a shower and went to bed, feeling better than she had the entire last year.

The next day Dahlia stood behind her chair at the salon, waiting on her client Jane to sit down in her chair. "Hey, Jane," she spoke as Jane plopped down in the chair.

"You seem tired," Jane said.

"I am, and I can't see a break any time in the near future."

"I wouldn't mind if I were you," she told Dahlia.

I know," Dahlia said. "It's been a lot of issues with the family, you know."

"Don't forget that your house is still waiting on you," Jane reminded.

"I know, Jane. I won't forget." Dahlia paused.

"I'm more upset that I paid for this trip to Jamaica and can't go," Jane vented. Dahlia stopped combing Jane's hair.

"What's wrong?" Jane asked. Dahlia's eyes watered up. "Come on, let's go outside," Jane offered and led Dahlia, not wanting the salon to see her at a weak point.

Once outside, Dahlia's tears rolled down her face. That was the first time she felt her tears since Mecca left. She explained everything that was going on with Smoke and Mecca and how he took their son to Jamaica. Her tears wouldn't stop coming as she talked—a year's worth of tears, all at once.

"Well, that settles it," Jane said. "You and whoever it is have a free trip to Jamaica."

"What?" Dahlia asked, not believing what she was hearing.

"I can't go...and you need to go, what else needs to be said?"

"But what..." Before she could finish her sentence, Jane cut her off.

"I hate wasting money. It really upsets me. Don't make me waste my money, Dahlia," she said as she walked back to the salon door, leaving her standing there. Dahlia followed. "Fix your face," she said to Dahlia before opening the door. "You look too pretty to be crying."

Dahlia quickly wiped the tears away from her face and went back into the salon. Jane didn't want to talk about the situation in the salon. So, she took Dahlia's number and promised to stop by her house to bring the tickets later. "You, my darling," Jane whispered in her ear while they hugged goodbye, "are one step closer to getting your son back, I can feel it."

Dahlia walked home with extra pep in her step. Jane's words left her feeling like she could conquer the world. What were the odds of Jane having these tickets and not being able to go. To Dahlia, it was a sign. What Jane whispered in her ear, had to be right. She made a stop at Roro's to tell her the news.

Jamaica sounded really tempting to Roro, and if it was under different circumstances, she would go. But this was strictly about Mecca, so they both felt it necessary for Dahlia to take her parents. She left and headed home, excited to break the good news to them. As soon as she walked in the house, she called them. She told her parents everything that Rodney told her and about the tickets to Jamaica that her client gave her. After her parents were caught up to speed, a very quick decision was made. Her, her mother and her father, were going to Jamaica.

Jane called Dahlia not long after she got off the bus to let her know that she was on her way to bring the tickets. Dahlia waited as patiently as she could and bolted out the door as soon as she saw Jane's car. The closer Dahlia got to the car, the more overwhelmed she felt. She was closer to being back united with Mecca than she ever thought possible. She knew that there was no way that she could ever repay her client.

When Jane stepped out of the car, she immediately grabbed Dahlia and hugged her. She looked around at the guys standing on the corner and the trash that littered the streets. Dahlia could tell that Jane didn't care too much for the neighborhood that she lived in.

"So, this is where you and little Mecca live?" she asked Dahlia as she looked around.

"Yes, this is where we live," Dahlia said. Jane smiled and changed the subject. She described the hotel that they would be staying in and other attractions available to her if she chose to take advantage on her trip. They talked a few minutes more before Jane told Dahlia that she had somewhere to go.

"Thank you so much, Jane."

"Anytime, sweetheart," Jane said and placed the tickets in Dahlia's hands. She hugged her one last time and got in her car and left.

Dahlia couldn't believe that she was holding three pieces of paper, that made it one step closer for her to hold

Mecca again. She walked in the house and called her parents again. It was happening! Dahlia and her parents were on their way to Jamaica! *"Mecca here we come!"*

CHAPTER 11

A Category Five

D ahlia and her parents finally touched down in Jamaica. Their lawyer advised after checking into the hotel that they immediately go to the police station. They were finally getting closer to holding Mecca, and they couldn't wait. Although they were actually in Jamaica, Dahlia couldn't let go of the negative feelings until she physically had Mecca in her arms.

Despite, everything seemed to be falling into place. Once they met with the police officers, they were surprised by how the officers treated them. They were very nice and respectful. Nothing like Dahlia pictured from the movies on tv. After giving the authorities all the information that

Rodney had given her, they assured Dahlia and her parents that they would handle the situation right away.

Now it was time for the waiting game. Although living without Mecca was the hardest thing in the world to do, waiting was not far under it. They did everything they could to stay productive, but it was hard...extremely hard. Being that the hotel that Jane booked was on the beach, Dahlia's parents decided to take advantage. They walked the beach to clear their minds. Dahlia on the other hand, stayed in the room, just in case the officers were to call. She couldn't see herself enjoying anything anyway, not without Mecca there to enjoy it with her.

Dahlia walked out onto the balcony. *"Jamaica is beautiful!"* she thought as she breathed in the fresh smell of saltwater, admiring how beautiful the water was. The water in Virginia looked so dirty in comparison. She wondered if Smoke and Kim ever took Mecca to the beach. She then pictured her and Mecca walking on that same beach, her holding his hand and him holding hers. The way he would look at her and smile....then she heard a knock on the door. Dahlia ran into the room as fast as she could to answer the door. She flung the door open and fell to her knees as tears rushed down her cheeks.

"Mommy!" Mecca yelled as he hugged her as tight as his little arms would allow. Dahlia couldn't speak, all she wanted to do was hold him. She heard the officers talking, but it was blurred. Her mind was clouded, but in a good way. Dahlia searched his body for bruises before being able to speak, "...Are you okay?" she asked.

"Ma'am," the officers repeated several times, until finally catching Dahlia's attention. "Ma'am, we have the child's father in custody. But we have one problem," they said and showed Dahlia a piece of paper. "Did you sign this?"

Dahlia read the paper and saw what seemed to be her signature. "No sir, I didn't agree for my son to leave the country."

"Well then, that's all we need. Thank you for your time," the officer said and walked away, leaving Dahlia and Mecca there alone to embrace one another.

Dahlia had so many questions, but she didn't want to put that pressure on Mecca right now. He had already been through too much, and now she just wanted to shower him with nothing but her love. As far as she was concerned, they had a lifetime to ask each other questions, and besides, he looked tired. "Come on Mecca, let mommy bath you and get you dressed for bed," she said as she picked him up.

She felt it would be a good way to inspect every inch of his body without making him think anything was wrong. She tried her hardest to shield him from the harsh reality of what really happened. Mecca laid his head down on his mother's shoulder as she carried him into the restroom. She teared up remembering that feeling. The feeling of his head laying on her shoulder and his face towards her neck, just as he always did. She briefly wondered if he also did the same thing with Kim. She felt a little jealous, reminding herself that he was going home now and that everything else was now the past.

After Dahlia bathed Mecca, it wasn't long before he was fast asleep. She laid him on her bed, excited that she had the opportunity to cuddle with him tonight. She sat beside him and stared for a moment. He seemed to have grown a little taller and was obviously well fed; she noticed he had gotten a little heavier.

Dahlia heard her parents as they entered the hotel room.

"Dahlia?" her mother called.

Dahlia quickly left the room where Mecca was sleeping because she didn't want to wake him up. She also thought it would be a good idea to surprise them.

"How's my baby girl?" her father asked, taking his daughter in his arms.

"I feel better, Daddy," she said.

"You and your dad should walk on the beach," Mrs. Dot recommended. "It's beautiful, I will wait on the police to call."

"No thanks, I don't want to go anywhere right now," Dahlia said.

"Okay." Mrs. Dot understood the pain her daughter was going through. She gave Dahlia a kiss on her forehead and walked towards the room where Mecca was laying. Once she entered and flicked the light on, she screamed, as if she'd seen a ghost. But instead of running back out, she yelled, "Thank you, GOD" over and over again.

Dahlia's father looked at Dahlia as if he was puzzled on why his wife was acting like that. He walked toward the room when he saw his wife walking out of the room carrying Mecca. Her father became weak and fell onto the floor, thanking GOD for everything that he's done. When he got off the floor, he walked over to his wife and cried as he held her, as she held Mecca. Dahlia became emotional watching them and put her arms around them both. They all stood around Mecca, with Mrs. Dot holding him, and cried.

The next morning, Dahlia took Mecca for a walk on the beach. She watched as he stomped the water with his feet. "Did you have fun with your dad Mecca?" she asked, looking away so he wouldn't feel uncomfortable answering.

"Yeah Mommy, I had fun with Daddy...did you enjoy being dead?" he asked.

"Dead?" Dahlia asked confused.

"Daddy and Mommy says that you're dead, and that's why I was with him... Did you have fun?" Mecca asked.

"Your mother isn't dead Mecca, and I'm your only mommy."

"No silly," Mecca replied explaining that he had another mommy also. Dahlia explained that she was very much alive the entire time, and that she was his only mother. Mecca looked at Dahlia confused. Dahlia didn't want to ask any more questions. She was afraid of saying the wrong thing and didn't want to make matters worse. She changed the subject, "Do you want to make a sandcastle?" she asked, knowing he'd say yes.

While they were building the sandcastle, Mecca mentioned how he made sandcastles with his Mommy while his dad swam.

"Mecca," Dahlia said, taking a deep breath. "I'm your only mommy. You have no other mommy, Mecca." He glanced at Dahlia briefly and went back to building on the sandcastle.

Dahlia's heart felt heavy. She couldn't believe that Smoke would take this so far. Not only did he steal Mecca taking him out of the country, but he had Mecca thinking that she was dead AND calling another woman mommy. There was no one she hated worse in the world. He had stooped to a new low. And only time would tell how much it had truly affected their son. She had to prepare herself for the constant corrections that she would now have to give Mecca for calling that bitch mommy. Kim would be better off staying in Jamaica because the way Dahlia felt, if she ever saw her again, she'd make sure Kim wished she didn't.

Later that day, Dahlia's parents treated her and Mecca out to eat. While Dahlia and her parents were carrying on a conversation, they noticed that Mecca stopped eating and sat there with his bottom lip poked out.

"What's wrong?" Dahlia's parents asked. Dahlia didn't ask or say anything. She was afraid to hear what his response was going to be. What happened at the beach earlier was enough for her.

Mecca looked up at his grandparents and started to cry. Dahlia's father quickly grabbed his grandson, holding him tight as he asked what was wrong again. Mecca cried harder...so hard that he couldn't speak and began hyperventilating.

After Dahlia's dad finally calmed Mecca down, Mrs.Dot asked Mecca again what was wrong with him.

"I miss my daddy," he whined.

"Awe," Mrs. Dot responded and rubbed Mecca's back. "You'll see your daddy again. Come to me." She took him from out of her husband's arms.

Dahlia was infuriated. Her eyes narrowed, getting redder by the second, and her hands began shaking. She tried her hardest to control it in front of her parents and Mecca. "I'll be right back," she said getting up from the table.

"I'm going to kill that bitch!" she mumbled as she pushed the bathroom door open as hard as she could without considering whether anyone was behind it. She just had to get away from everyone, to calm herself down.

Dahlia looked at herself in the long mirror that hung over the bathroom sink. She noticed how red her eyes were. She's been noticing that happening lately whenever she gets angry. If Roro was here, she knew that they never would've gave the police the information that she did. They probably would've gotten Mecca back, but saved the information, just so she could kick Kim's ass like she wanted to do now. She then considered how they were in Kim's country, with Kim's family, and their local laws. She'd have a large advantage. "I wonder how that would've turned out," Dahlia thought, a question that she really didn't have to ask herself, because she already knew. One thing was for certain—it wouldn't have been pretty.

CHAPTER 12

A Winter Storm

Roro sat on her front porch on a Sunday afternoon looking down the street, watching to make sure Mrs. Pat didn't pull up early after church and catch Mr. Chris drinking in her house.

"Damn Mr. Chris, the fuck you doing in there?" she asked, rushing him to come outside. Mr. Chris came outside with an empty 40 ounce bottle. He walked towards the trashcan and lifted the top.

"Hold up, Chris, you know damn well that you don't throw that shit in my momma's trashcan! The fuck you doing...tryna get me fucked up?" she asked and pointed to her neighbor's trashcan.

"Damn, I almost forgot my girl," he said then put the lid back down on the trash can. "I'll see you next week." He waved and started walking away.

"Okay, Mr. Chris, see you next week," Roro responded and walked back into the house.

Roro loved Sundays because Mrs. Pat always took Jeremiah to church with her and that left the house to herself. She rolled a blunt and walked up the street to one of her cousin's house.

"June," she yelled, banging on her cousin's screen door. "Open the damn door!"

"Wait a minute!" June yelled back. She slowly walked to the door and let Roro in.

"I mean, what the fuck?" Roro said, "...you might as well leave the motherfucker open. I'm over here around the same time every damn day anyway."

June looked at Roro from the corner of her eyes. "Bitch, your gonna stop cussing in my house too."

"Man, fuck yo house," Roro said as she lit up the blunt.

"Okay, bitch keep it up," June said smiling.

"I wonder what the fuck is going on with Dahlia, and Mecca right now." She inhaled deeply and passed June the blunt.

"Shit, she good," June said as she held the smoke in, releasing it through her nose after her first puff. She started coughing instantly trying to release, so bad that she just handed the blunt right back to Roro.

"Amateur," Roro joked as she snatched the blunt from her cousin's hand.

"All I can say," June continued, this time with a clear voice. "...no news is good news."

"Real shit," Roro said as she held the smoke in, also releasing it through her nose. And just like her cousin, she started coughing. June looked at Roro and laughed.

She snatched the blunt out of Roro's hand, "...Fucking amateur." That time, she hit the blunt like a pro.

"By the way Cuzzo, what's up with your boy Jason?" June asked.

"Ain't shit up with his ass, I told you what happened that night at the club right?" Roro retold June everything that happened at the club and at Social Services. "I haven't heard from that nigga since. He haven't even checked on Jeremiah, after getting knocked the fuck out...asshole!"

June got angry the more she thought about what her cousin went through that night. "Girl, I still can't believe that you never let the family know that that pussy motherfucker hit you... and now you got me wondering how many times he's done that shit before. If you didn't make me feel like I would have to whip yo ass, then I would've most definitely said something," June said as she passed Roro the blunt back.

Roro looked at June with a smirk on her face, "...Yeah, picture that."

Roro decided to come clean with her cousin. "To be honest...yes we did have a few fights. But in actuality, that motherfucker can't handle me for real. He'll never be able to handle me. He's a man, and that goes without saying. But when shit really hits the fan...just put it like this," Roro paused hitting the blunt, "...that bitch already know that I'm not wrapped to tight."

June couldn't do nothing but agree. Everyone that knew Roro knew that much. No one was going to put their hands on her and walk around like life was good. That goes for family members, friends or even the police. Jeremiah didn't even put his hands on his mother after finding out the hard way at an early age. June accepted Roro's explanation and changed the subject.

After sitting and talking with June for a few hours, Roro decided to head home. She had a few phone calls to make and felt the need to escape after telling her about Jason. She told her everything she wanted to tell her and didn't want to talk anymore. Roro knew if her family got a whiff of what happened at the club, shit would hit the fan. That's not what she, nor Jason wanted. Besides, she had always been able to take care of herself, every since she was a child. She had to, being one of only a few women in her male-dominated family. They made sure that all of their girl cousins were able to handle themselves.

Roro opened the door and sat on the couch and picked up the phone to handle some business, starting with the most important.

"Hello Jay! What's up?"

"Hey, baby girl," he answered. She could tell that he was both surprised and happy that she called. "What's going on with you?"

"Nothing really," she answered,"...just calling to say hello." Roro really didn't have much to say. She was really calling to see if he would answer, and to feel him out because her girl was in his country. If anyone would know anything, it would be him. After all, he is Kim's brother.

Roro searched her mind for a valid way to pry about if he had heard anything about what was going on without blowing her cover. She wasn't good at because he immediately caught on.

"Your sister got her son back again," he said.

"Oh, she did?!" Roro answered, enthusiastic about seeing her and Mecca again. She could no longer hide her emotions and questioned him about everything that came to mind.

Jay answered everything to the best of his ability, even giving extra information. "Look...me nor did my family really know the truth about everything that happened. We were under the impression that Smoke had won custody of his son and that his life was threatened. That was supposed to have been the reason they left." He went on to tell Roro that Kim didn't know, and that she was only going on what Smoke had told her.

Even though she was surprised to hear him say that about his sister, Roro didn't respond. She didn't know what Kim had told him, but she was more than aware that Kim was inside the courtroom when the judge awarded Dahlia custody of Mecca. The less he knew, the better. She didn't know who the bad guys were. She just knew that she was going to keep him and his crew as comfortable as she could. So, if Kim ever decided to come back to Norfolk or anywhere near Virginia, Roro was going to fuck her ass up.

After Jay felt that he said enough to prove his sister's innocence, he asked Roro what she was doing later. She didn't know how to answer. She knew how her mouth could be, so she tried her hardest to control what came out. What she really wanted to say was "Hell naw, fuck you and your sister, and by the way when is she coming back, so I can whip her ass."

Instead, she explained to him that she had made plans with her son. "So, tonight wouldn't be a good time."

"Okay," he replied, understanding that Jeremiah came first. "When would you be available?"

"I don't know, I'll keep you in the loop," she said, thinking of a reason to get off the phone. "I'm going to call you back, my mom is pulling up with Jeremiah now."

"Okay, let me know when you're free. Bye," Jay said and hung up the phone.

Roro checked on the beef stew that her mother had put in the crockpot before she left out of the house for church. After confirming it was done, she cut off the crockpot. She put some in a bowl and turned on the television. "Oh shit, Good Times is on." She made herself comfortable in a chair to enjoy.

Roro loved that show a lot because it somehow reminded her of her and her female cousins. "I'm Thelma," they all used to say, trying to be the first to pick which cast members that they wanted to be. The episode that they played that day though, was one that Roro didn't particularly care for. It was the one when Penny's mother broke her arm.

Roro thought back to a babysitter that used to watch her while her mother worked. The babysitter never physically abused her, just allowed her kids to. That was a decision that she (the babysitter) would soon regret.

The sitter would always act extremely nice when her mother was around, but as soon as Mrs. Pat left, Moonie (the babysitter), would act the complete opposite.

Moonie was a single mother and had five kids of her own. She had three girls and two boys. Out of the five were a set of identical twins, the same age as Roro. In fact, at the time, one of them was in Roro's first grade class. Roro didn't know the ages of Moonie's other three kids, she just knew that they were teenagers.

By Roro being the only child, it seemed to the other kids that Roro had everything, which didn't make Moonie too happy. Roro remembered listening to Moonie talk about her to her friends, and not one single adult standing up for her. As an adult, Roro couldn't understand that because these women had kids of their own.

Roro remembered that it was one of the older girls' birthday, and she had a few friends over. She remembered the older sister making one of her younger siblings fight Roro, trying to show her friends how strong her siblings were. After the older sister realized that her younger sister was no match for Roro, she forced the other twin to jump in, while her and her friends watched like it was entertainment, laughing the entire time.

When Roro went to Moonie with a bloodied nose, crying about what happened, Moonie didn't say a word. She took Roro to the bathroom, cleaned her nose, and made her take a nap. That was one of many things that Roro endured with that babysitter. She never told Mrs. Pat what was going on, because she felt like she would be the one to get in trouble.

The constant picking and bullying started to change Roro. She became insensitive to things that she usually showed empathy for. She also started bullying other kids herself. Any signs of weakness she had begun to wither away. Mrs. Pat constantly called to check in with the school, but the whippings that Mrs. Pat gave Roro only made her stronger.

One day Mrs. Pat dropped Roro off at the babysitter's house before work as usual. Roro decided to bring her rubik's cube, this time, daring one of the twins to snatch it from her. As planned, one of the twins snatched the rubik's cube. Roro snatched it back as hard as she could. Like clockwork, the twins came at Roro swinging.

Roro no longer wanted to be the victim and did everything possible to win. She didn't know what happened during the fight, rage took over. All Roro remembered was the older sister pushing her back off of her younger sister. The younger twin laid on the ground crying, while the other twin cried, holding her arm.

It turned out that in the midst of the fight, Roro had bit a chunk out of one twins' arm, and never stopped punching the other one until she was pulled off of them by their older sister. That fight changed the way Roro moved through life. Never would she be anyone else's victim. And never would those kids, the twins nor the older sister ever pick on her again.

CHAPTER 13

Sleet

It was a good day for Roro. Her partner in crime, Dahlia, was on her way home. Roro couldn't wait to see Little Mecca. Dahlia had been in Jamaica for a week now, and hopefully she would be less stressed. While Roro had never been to Jamaica, she had heard a lot of stories about it and they all sounded good. *"Hopefully Dahlia got a few numbers from some heavy hitters,"* she thought as she held Jeremiah's hand as they walked toward the daycare.

Before Roro dropped Jeremiah off, she reminded him of the same thing that she did every day. "If any of them bad ass kids hit you, you better hit they asses back." She gave him a kiss and left to catch the next bus to work.

Even though she would tell him that every day, Roro didn't have to worry about Jeremiah. She and Jason had taught Jeremiah at an early age how to defend himself. She never let him run from anyone, even as a baby, no matter how big the other child was. Boy nor girl, it didn't matter to Roro. If you put your hands on Jeremiah, she was going to make sure that he had the last hit. That goes without saying, that at the precious age of four, Jeremiah has already been in more fights than most women. And because of that, so had Roro.

As soon as Roro and Jeremiah got off the bus, instead of walking home, they walked straight to Dahlia's house. Before knocking, Roro put her ear to the door to see if she could hear any kind of movement. "Yes, the tv is on," she said aloud, happy to hear some life in her friend's house.

Dahlia's neighbor walked outside quickly to let Roro know that her friend was home.

"What the fuck?" Dahlia yelled, irritated. "Did I ask you for any information? Get off her fucking dick! You watch everything that's going on over here, bitch, she don't have nothing that you want...trust me." She turned back to the door and knocked.

The neighbor was surprised by her reaction. "First of all, I never knew that she had a dick."

"I know your ass know she doesn't, because you know everything, with your nosey ass. Shoo fly shoo." Roro waved him off as Dahlia opened her door.

"Disrespectful," the neighbor said loudly as he walked back toward his door.

"So is that thick crust around your lips, be nosey about that," Roro said before walking into Dahlia's house.

"What in the hell is going on out here?" Dahlia asked and peeped out the door.

"Nothing that a little hot water and lotion won't clear up," Roro said laughing. "Hey, my friend," she paused to hug Dahlia, "Where is he?" She walked in the living room looking around.

"He's in his room...I feel like I already need a mental break."

Roro jumped up and ran towards her precious Mecca.

"Girl," Dahlia called after Roro.

Before Dahlia could say anything, Roro reappeared disappointed, "... he's sleep."

"Girl and I'm more than thankful." Dahlia explained everything that happened in Jamaica to Roro, including the things Mecca told her.

Roro listened to Dahlia talk about everything that Smoke did in disbelief. Not that she didn't believe her friend, but the whole situation was surprising to Roro. She wouldn't have expected this from him in a million years. "Now I'm stuck in between a rock and a hard place," Dahlia explained. "My son is taking this harder than I expected. I do love him as far as being Mecca's father, so I don't want him to go to prison."

That statement confused Roro in the worse way. She was going to have Dahlia's back regardless, but this nigga took Mecca away from them for a whole year. "Fuck him!" Roro blurted. "That dude ain't Smoke no more. The Smoke that I knew wouldn't have stooped so damn low. He's grimy as hell." Roro could see the impact that all of this was having on her friend. She started to tear up as she listened to her continue her story.

Roro got Dahlia caught up on everything that had happened when she was gone. They laughed and joked for a while and once it started getting dark, Roro headed home.

"I'm so happy that you and Mecca are home safe." Roro hugged Dahlia one last time before leaving.

"Me too," Dahlia responded, hugging Roro as hard as she could. "I'll see you tomorrow."

When Roro left, she was startled by some strange man sitting on Dahlia's neighbor's porch.

"Hi, how are you?" the guy asked, noticing Roro staring at him.

"Hi," she responded. She could also see someone's shadow, peeking out of his blinds. *"They are either paranoid as a bitch in that motherfucker, or they are looking out for the police, because all the drug dealers must be hanging out over there,"* she thought as her and Jeremiah continued to walk home. She couldn't wait to get to her bed.

The next morning after Roro got dressed, she walked in the kitchen and saw Jeremiah already sitting at the table eating breakfast. Mrs. Pat helped Roro out a lot with Jeremiah. A few of the things were getting him dressed and fed every morning that Roro had to work at the shop.

"Good morning," Roro said to Mrs. Pat as she hugged her from behind then sat at the table with Jeremiah.

"Good morning, how are you?" Mrs. Pat asked as she touched Roro's arm. "How's my girl Dahlia, and little Mecca doing...let her know that, I don't appreciate her not bringing my baby around here to see me yesterday."

"Oh, Ma!" Roro said and began telling her mother everything that Dahlia had told her.

"Oh, poor baby," Mrs. Pat responded, watching Jeremiah stuff his mouth with food. "Stop stuffing your mouth before you choke. You're acting like you never ate before." Mrs. Pat then turned to Dahlia, "She'll be fine.

He's young, and this is still new. He'll get over this." She got up from the table to wash out her plate.

"I hope you're right, Momma," Roro said as she grabbed Jeremiah's plate and passed it to her. Roro walked across the street to June's house to smoke a blunt before work, like she did every morning. After talking and joking with June for a while, she asked June what time it was.

"It's 8:30," June said, looking at Dahlia like she was crazy.

"Bitch why didn't you tell me the time?" Roro asked.

"Man, you're in control of your own shit." June shook her head. "You say the same shit every day, knowing that you have to work."

"So, bitch. Fuck you." Roro ran out June's door and back to her mother's to get Jeremiah.

She ran down the street as fast as Jeremiah's little legs would let him go. She saw Dahlia standing near the bus stop, looking down the street in her direction.

"The bus is coming," Dahlia yelled at her. Roro couldn't respond, she was out of breath. She picked Jeremiah up so she could run faster.

By the time Roro reached the bus stop she looked down the street, to see no bus at all. Instead, she saw Dahlia laughing like her mind had gone bad. "Fuck," Roro said, looking at Dahlia like she could kill her.

Dahlia kept laughing, "I couldn't help but make a joke out of it...I know you want to say fuck me don't you...bitch catch your breath first."

"Fuck you," Roro said, still trying to catch her breath and letting out a little laughter.

"Bitch, yo ass is always late, that shit don't make no fucking sense. You know that you don't have to smoke every damn morning, forcing poor little Jeremiah into a track star before kindergarten, don't you?" Dahlia asked.

Roro, finally in control of her breath looked at Dahlia, "I feel ya bitch...but my morning smoke is what helps keep me mentally grounded throughout the day."

"I feel you." Dahlia understood everything that Roro had gone through. She knew more about Roro's life than Mrs. Pat. Roro knew Dahlia wouldn't tell a soul, that's why they trusted each other. Their friendship was rare; the people around them just didn't know how deep it really was.

After Roro and Dahlia dropped Jeremiah off at daycare, they caught the next bus. Roro sat by the window and Dahlia took the outer seat. They laughed and joked as people got on and off. Roro glanced out the window and her eyes became big as saucers at the same time that Dahlia glanced at her.

"What's wrong?" Dahlia asked, looking out the window in the direction Roro was staring.

"Gina," Dahlia said under her breath, but loud enough for Roro to hear her.

Roro looked at Dahlia, "Fuck that bitch. We'll see her ass again, and she won't be in her car at a stoplight, and we won't be on the bus...trust me."

Dahlia looked out the bus window for Gina's car every day for three weeks straight after Roro's comment, hoping to see Gina's car parked anywhere, it didn't matter if it was near the salon, she would still get off the bus. She hadn't seen her since that day.

A couple of weeks later, Dahlia only had a few appointments and decided to help Roro by shampooing a few of Roro's clients in between her own appointments. Roro was running wild trying to work with each client. By the time they got off, Roro was beat. So beat, that Dahlia told Roro to sit at the bus stop while she went and got Jeremiah from the daycare.

Roro planned to take Jeremiah home and go to Dahlia's house, but she was too tired. Instead, she opted to go home and get some sleep. "I'm going to call you later sis, I'm tired as hell."

"I know you are," Dahlia said. "Your ass is always busy at work. Call me when you wake up."

"Okay, I got you," Roro said as her and Jeremiah walked through Rodney's group of friends.

"Yo," they yelled as she walked through them. Roro was in no mood to entertain their foolishness. She just kept walking as if she didn't hear them. She was used to it. They've been doing that since they started hanging out there. Roro understood that even though she had been living in the neighborhood for years, they looked at her as the new girl, and with her attitude, she knew it was possible that she would wound up having to cut one of them motherfuckers.

When Roro hit the door, she spoke to her mother and went straight into the shower. After she got out of the shower she laid in her bed and cut the tv in her room on. Within minutes, Roro was sound asleep.

Roro stood in Dahlia's kitchen cooking, laying out the bacon on the paper towel as she heard Dahlia let out a hurling scream. Roro ran into Dahlia's room as fast as she could. Upon entering the room, she saw Dahlia holding a gun, pointing it towards someone laying on the floor. Roro tried to get a better view to see who the person was but couldn't. The more she focused, the more blurred the person became. The only thing she could tell was that it was a man.

"Is he dead?" Roro asked. Dahlia didn't respond nor did she look in Roro's direction. It was as if Roro wasn't there. Roro kept asking Dahlia is he dead and what was going on. Dahlia never answered, she just looked at the strange man, laying on her floor.

"Mommy," Jeremiah yelled as he jumped on the bed, waking his mother out of a nightmare. "Mommy can you walk me to the store," he asked, excited that one of Mrs. Pat's friends from church had given him a dollar. Roro looked toward her bedroom window, noticing she had slept for hours because it was now dark outside. "What time is it?" she asked Jeremiah, as if he knew how to tell time.

"It's 13 o'clock," he answered, happy that someone had finally asked him a grown up question.

Roro chuckled as she looked at her clock hanging on the wall. *"Damn, it's 10:00 already,"* she thought to herself, not wanting to burst Jeremiah's bubble. "Okay thanks

Jeremiah, I don't know what I'd do without you." She kissed him on his forehead. "But 13 o'clock, is definitely too late to be walking to anybody's store."

She walked inside the restroom to brush her teeth. While Roro brushed her teeth, she heard someone banging on the door. "What the fuck?" she said aloud, forgetting her mother was home.

"Watch your mouth," Mrs. Pat yelled, acknowledging she heard her.

"Who is it?" Mrs. Pat yelled. Roro peeped out the bathroom door.

"Hey, Chris," Mrs. Pat said as she opened the door.

"Mr. Chris, I know his ass saw Momma's car outside. See, now I'd be wrong if I cuss his ass out!" Roro thought as she rinsed the mouthwash out of her mouth. *"That nigga's trying to set me up."* She finished in the bathroom and walked toward the door.

"Noo!" Roro could hear Mrs. Pat yell, which propelled her to walk faster.

"What's going on, Ma?" Dahlia asked frantically!

"I don't know," Mrs. Pat answered. "Get Jeremiah, we have to go to Dahlia's house."

Roro began to replay the dream that she just had in her head. She couldn't think of anything but her friend. She bolted out of the door; she knew that she had to get there, and fast. Her mother's car wasn't faster than her own legs in the moment. Before she came across Dahlia's street, she could see the red and blue lights reflecting from the stop sign.

Roro replayed the dream again, this time, switching the roles. She pictured Dahlia laying on the floor, and the guy holding the gun. To Roro that seemed more accurate. Roro couldn't stop running. Once she reached Dahlia's street, she could see police cars and lights as far as her eyes could reach.

"No, No, No," she repeated over and over again until she reached her destination.

Roro lifted the yellow tape and tried to run inside of Dahlia's house, when one of the officers grabbed her. "Nooo!" she yelled and hit the officer with all of her might. The officer stumbled back from the sudden blow, then grabbed her again, this time with more reinforcement. More officers came as Roro began swinging wildly. She just knew that she had to get in that house, and now.

Roro could hear Mrs. Pat in the background calling her name but couldn't respond. To her, she didn't think that her mother would understand. Something happened to her best friend. Someone just killed her best friend, and these officers were going to stop her from entering that house.

"That's her friend," Roro could hear someone from the crowd of onlookers yelling at the officers.

"That's her sister," someone else yelled. "Let her go," she could hear them yelling as she fell to the ground and her hands were being pulled behind her. Dahlia felt the coldness from the handcuffs as it clicked around her wrist.

As they picked her up and walked her to the car, she couldn't talk. She could see Mrs. Pat talking to the officers, trying to explain her daughter's actions. Roro shook her head as one of the officers placed her in the car and shut the door. Roro replayed the dream again, not as it originally happened, but the way she felt like it did. Only this time the roles would be reversed again. It was her best friend and four year old nephew laid out on the floor. She had to get out of that police car. Dahlia laid on her back and began kicking the car's window. She had to escape. She had to see her friend.

The last kick seemed successful, because she couldn't feel anything else there, so she sat up to plan her escape and fight again to enter Dahlia's house. When she sat up, she saw three officers standing beside Mrs. Pat.

"Mommy!" Roro yelled as tears flew from her eyes. "Mommy!" It was the only word she could say. The officers had noticed her attempt to kick out the window, and opened the door to let her out of the back of the police car. Mrs. Pat grabbed her daughter immediately, held her and began to pray.

One of the officers began explaining some of the details, while Dahlia was inside talking to the detectives. As the officer told them everything that he was allowed to, they saw them bring the lifeless body out in a body bag. *"I wonder who the fuck that is,"* Roro thought. Roro couldn't believe what her eyes were showing her.

"It's not the occupant of the house," the officer quickly responded, but revealed that someone had indeed been killed.

Roro looked at the officer, feeling more relieved. "Where is her son?"

"It's only the young lady that lives here, there are no children involved," the officer answered.

Roro let out a big sigh, at the same time as Mrs. Pat yelled out, "THANK YOU JESUS!"

Roro immediately turned her attention back to the officer. "Dahlia didn't do it! She's not that type of a person. She's not even the fighting type. So when are y'all going to let her go?" Roro asked.

The officer couldn't answer that question. "Ma'am, your friend is inside talking with the detectives now. We're trying to wrap this up as fast as we can."

"Answer the question sir," Roro said irritated.

"Roro," Mrs. Pat said looking at her only child. "Let them do their job. Then we can talk to Dahlia and see what's going on."

Roro seemed to understand that a little better. She looked at the officer, "Now take these fucking handcuffs off of me!"

"Okay ma'am, but you have to promise me that you can control yourself and let us get to the bottom of all of this."

"Sure," Roro answered.

When the officer finally took the handcuffs off of Roro, her and Mrs. Pat went back to Mrs. Pat's car and sat with

Mr. Chris and Jeremiah. Everyone in the car was quiet, except Mrs. Pat, who continued to pray the entire time. "God got her," she assured them. "She's going to be alright. Once he's in the midst of things, it's nothing that anyone can do."

Roro looked out the car window and up at the sky. She remembered when her and Dahlia were young, laying in Dahlia's grandparents back yard looking up at the stars. That was always soothing to Dahlia. As she stared at the stars now, Roro felt a sense of peace. *"It's something magical going on up there,"* she mumbled to herself. Roro looked to her side and saw Jeremiah watching her. She sat him on her lap and hugged him tightly as she cried.

"I have to call her parents," Mrs. Pat said, looking in the back seat at Roro. "I can't leave you here, you have to come with me."

Roro understood the reason her mom said that, and agreed.

"Can I use your restroom Mr. Chris asked?" Roro knew that the beer was starting to run through him.

"You sure can," Mrs. Pat responded. She went on to thank him for letting them know what was going on at Dahlia's house.

As Mrs. Pat drove toward the house, Roro saw Gina's car riding past. *"A nosey bitch,"* she thought, as she watched Gina look down Dahlia's street, driving slow. Roro wanted to jump out of the car, but Mrs. Pat and Jeremiah were inside. *"You keep riding past my girls house, I'm going to see you bitch,"* she thought to herself as she watched Gina drive faster once she seen that Dahlia's house was surrounded by police cars. Mrs. Pat and Mr. Chris went in the house while Roro and Jeremiah waited in the car.

Roro's mind wandered as she tried to put the pieces together. *"Dahlia just left Jamaica after getting Mecca back. Gina and Kim are best friends. It's a dead person being brought out of Dahlia's house."*

"Bitch!" Roro yelled. "If I find out that you were involved, I'm going to jail." Roro didn't realize she was talking loud.

"No Mommy," Jeremiah yelled crying. "I don't want you to go to jail."

"I'm not going to jail," Roro said quickly, trying to console him. Roro looked up and saw both Mrs. Pat and Mr. Chris coming out of the house. The last thing she wanted was for Mrs. Pat to see Jeremiah crying. And God forbid that he would have told her what he had just heard her say. She had to shut him up, and fast.

"Shut up!" she yelled at him. "Stop being a punk! I told you that I'm not going to jail, and that's the end of it!" The thought of him crying made her even more upset. "And if I were to go to jail, then what? You would become a little punk? Hell naw, stop that shit now!" she demanded as she wiped the tears from his eyes with the bottom of her shirt.

"Her parents are on the way," Mrs. Pat said as her and Mr. Chris got in the car. "Are you okay?" Mrs. Pat asked Roro.

"Yes ma'am, I'm okay," Roro answered. Dahlia looked at Jeremiah, and watched as he stared at her. He nodded his head, and she smiled and nodded back. She understood then that for the first time, everything she was teaching him was starting to sink in. "That's my boy," she told him, pulling him closer to her.

Dahlia's parents arrived at Dahlia's house in no time. They tried to enter the house but the officers wouldn't allow it. Mrs. Pat got out of her car and walked over to them. Roro didn't want to get out of the car because she knew that Mrs. Dot was going to cry, and Roro didn't want to see that. She hated the feeling of sadness; it made her feel as if she was weak, and she couldn't get with that.

When Mrs. Dot started crying Roro made sure that she turned her head and looked straight ahead, avoiding looking in her direction. She was in control of what she chose to remember, and that wasn't going to be a part.

Roro thought of how strong her mother was. She was happy that it was Mrs. Pat that was able to talk to Mrs. Dot, and not her. She also thought of how much respect she had for Mrs. Dot and how she loved her no nonsense attitude; Mrs. Dot played no games. It kind of reminded her of how she would be once she reached that age. So, seeing her vulnerable was hard and not an option.

Roro watched Mrs. Dot talk to the officers and decided it was best to try and find out as much information about what was going on while she could, while Mr. Chris was still in the car, because she knew that it was only a matter of time before he had to release. Besides, Mecca was in Dahlia's parents car alone, so she had to get him.

Roro slowly walked towards them, she was somewhat afraid to hear what was happening, but she knew that she had to know. Her arrival was almost perfect. She was able to hear everything that she needed to hear to piece it all together. Her heart dropped as she quickly turned and walked toward Mecca. She gently held her hand out as he held his arms out to her. She held him close as she carried him to Mrs. Pat's car with her. After hugging Mecca for as long as he allowed her to, she sat him in between her and Jeremiah. She stared at him, wondering what he was thinking. *"Only if he understood what was going on right now,"* she thought.

After sitting and waiting to speak with Dahlia for hours, Dahlia's front door finally opened. Roro noticed a police car drive up and park right in front of Dahlia's door. She opened her car door and stood outside the car. She watched two police officers bringing her sister and best friend out of the house. This time it would be Dahlia and not her walking out in handcuffs. The worst part of it all, was that it wasn't for assault...but for murder. Yet, the worst part of it all was yet to come. How in the hell do you explain to a four-year-old that his mother just killed his father.

CHAPTER 14

Freezing Rain

It had been a little over a year since Dahlia's arrest. The day for her trial finally had arrived. Roro rushed around the house searching for her shoe that Jeremiah had more than likely hidden. He would do that from time to time when he didn't want her to leave the house.

"Jeremiah, where is my shoe?" Roro asked searching around the house. She was trying to make sure she was ready when Dahlia's parents arrived. She didn't want to be late, nevertheless make them late.

"Oh, I found it," she said, after looking in Jeremiah's toy box. "Jeremiah, you're going to have to leave my stuff alone." She quickly finished doing everything she needed to do. The only thing she forgot to do was empty out her purse in search of anything incriminating before having to go through the metal detectors. She always felt more comfortable leaving her purse in the car anyway because it would be just her luck that she would overlook something, and that would be her ass.

Roro was getting restless, so she decided to wait outside on the porch. She knew that it wouldn't make things go any faster, but it made her feel like it would. Roro had very little patience and it showed. She expected immediate results, even in the most impossible circumstances. She attributed it to her mother always wanting to be early for everything. Which wasn't a bad thing, but having to sit and wait for appointments, or stores to open, was downright irritating to her. Roro told herself at a young age that when she became a woman, she would only get to her appointments five minutes early, versus a half hour. She would also go to the store, after they had already been opened for at least an hour. It may have made her late for a lot of things, but the way she looked at it, she didn't have to wait.

Roro finally saw Dahlia's parents' car coming up the street. She walked across the street so that all she had to do was jump in the backseat. Roro jumped in the car and spoke to Dahlia's parents.

"I see you're on time this morning huh?" Mrs. Dot joked.

"Yes ma'am, I can't be late today," Roro responded. "How's Mecca?"

"Oh he's doing fine," Mrs. Dot assured her. "I appreciate everything you and your mom do to help." She turned around in her seat so she could see Roro's face.

"No problem...we love him, he's our baby too," Roro said, meaning every word of it. "Besides, I don't trust anyone else with him and Jeremiah. And to be honest, I don't want to go to jail."

Mrs. Dot couldn't help but laugh at Roro's response, "I know baby." She smiled. Roro reminded her so much of her younger self. Now that Mrs. Dot was older and more calm, she was one of the few people that understood Roro.

When they walked in the courtroom, Roro immediately got a funny feeling as she followed Dahlia's parents all the way toward the front, to make it easier for Dahlia to see them. Roro hated being at the courthouse, or anywhere in its vicinity. Mainly, it was that she didn't like being surrounded by the police, but today, she hated that Dahlia's life was in the hands of people that didn't even know her. If they did know her, Dahlia would've been released...better yet, she wouldn't have been arrested in the first place.

Roro still couldn't believe the way things were panning out. *"I mean, why is Dahlia really behind bars? That nigga needed to die,"* Roro thought as she looked around the courtroom searching for his family and friends. *"They better not say no slick ass shit to me neither."* Once she located a few of his family members, sitting towards the back of the courtroom, she got mad all over again, *"I'll be locked up in this bitch with my homegirl,"* she told herself.

One thing she noticed did catch her off guard though. She saw Dahlia's next door neighbor sitting beside his family. What was even crazier, was that in between his family was the guy that she saw sitting on Dahlia's neighbors porch that night. *"This shit is about to get real,"* she thought to herself as she stared at them.

Roro tapped Dahlia's parents on their shoulder. "I knew that he couldn't be trusted," she whispered to them as she pointed to Dahlia's neighbor. *"What is his ass even doing here? Dahlia didn't do shit wrong, she was just protecting herself and her son, so what could he even possibly have to say. I do know one thing,"* she thought to herself. *"I'm kicking his ass when we leave."*

It was hard for Roro to think of everything Dahlia had experienced that night — having to actually kill someone. Roro looked at herself as somewhat of a gangsta. But she, herself, never had to cross that line before. She thought about all of the signs she saw, proving that Dahlia was turning into a thug...including her and Terri's fight. Dahlia progressed to the street life overnight.

Roro stood up for the judge as he finally approached the bench. There were so many unanswered questions that Roro needed answered. She couldn't wait to talk to Dahlia whenever she would be released and finally home. It was impossible to ask or say anything during their visits on video and recorded phone calls. Everything about this situation was foggy.

Roro and Dahlia's parents listened to the prosecutor paint Dahlia as a monster. They talked about how she made a false report that Smoke kidnapped Mecca, and that she knew that he was taking their son to Jamaica. They also listened to Dahlia's neighbor talk about how Smoke was constantly coming to her house and claimed they were still together. The guy that Roro saw sitting on Dahlia's neighbors porch built on that story by admitting that he himself had brought him there almost every day for the last week of his life.

Out of everything that was said in the courtroom, that stuck out to Dahlia more than anything. She knew her friend and could damn near piece the story together herself, even though she wasn't physically there. She knew that Smoke had to have been on some dumb shit for this shit to have taken place. But now, he was dealing with a different Dahlia, and couldn't get by with the same things he had in the past. If she was a monster now, it was one that he had created.

***

Everything about that night had left Roro cloudy. Even a year later, after the trial was well past over, she had just stopped looking for Dahlia's neighbor to kick his ass for testifying. She still never told anyone but Dahlia about the weird dream they both had that night when Dahlia went to jail. She felt as if she had told anyone else, they would've deemed her crazy and two screws loose of a coocoo's nest. Not that she cared about what anyone thought, but she almost felt she was crazy; that dream made her question her own sanity.

Roro remembered clear as day what happened when she told Dahlia about her dream. Dahlia also told Roro about a previous similar dream she had before the shooting.

"I can't believe it, Roro!" Dahlia had said. "You're the person that I heard in my dream running from my kitchen. I never saw you, but I definitely heard you."

Roro told Dahlia how she looked at her in the dream and how Dahlia never looked at her. She felt in the dream that Dahlia couldn't see her. *"What are the odds of that?"* they both wondered. That was their confirmation that blood doesn't make you family because their bond was as solid as any sisterly bond.

When Dahlia went to jail, it was hard on Mecca. Mrs. Dot made sure that she got him a good therapist because losing two parents in one night was too much for a young kid. Roro had already planned to step up to the plate. She and Mrs. Pat kept Mecca throughout the week to help Dahlia's parents while they worked. Dahlia nor Mrs. Pat considered it as babysitting, even refusing money. They considered Mecca as one of their own and didn't see a need to stop just because Dahlia was sentenced to ten years in prison.

The only difference was that they didn't have to take care of Mecca financially because Dahlia's parents provided him that. At the same time, if they saw anything he wanted or needed, they never hesitated to buy it.

Especially Roro, she was all for dressing Mecca and Jeremiah alike whenever she could. People that didn't really know her, or hadn't seen her in years, thought she had two sons and she never corrected it. She had even began to feel like she had two boys.

Roro decided to work a little more that week, to make a little extra since school would be starting in a couple of weeks. She didn't want to procrastinate too much... at least not when it came to this. Her job was not that far from Military Circle Mall, so it was easier for her to shop whenever she got off.

One particular day, Roro decided to walk in JANAF Shopping Center and browse through their stores to see what she could find for the boys. Thankfully, her mother was at the eye doctor in the same shopping center. She didn't mind catching the bus but it was always better whenever a ride came along.

She heard a few people talking about a children's clothing store called Kids Rainbow, so she decided to try it out. Maybe she could get more clothes than what she usually gets from the mall; she was told that they were pretty cheap. As Dahlia stood by a rack of clothes, searching for the boys' clothing size, she felt someone tap her on her shoulder. She turned around and saw Terri and her boyfriend standing behind her.

"Oh wow, hey!" Roro said. "How have you been? I haven't seen you in a long time." What she really wanted to say was that she hadn't seen Terri since Dahlia whooped her ass, but didn't. She didn't feel the need to remind her. Hopefully, she learned from getting her ass beat not to fuck with people that she deemed as weak. And that everyone has a breaking point.

"Hey!" Terri responded. She reached out and hugged her. "I've been doing good...just tryna get this school shopping out the way." Terri's boyfriend, aware of how much she loved to talk, continued walking, leaving them there to talk alone while he finished shopping for their kids. "Girl, what have you been up to lately?" Terri asked.

"Not a damn thing, girl," Roro answered. "Just work and home." Without coming out saying it, Roro was hinting to Terri that she was too busy to talk right now and she wouldn't be stopping by her house any time soon. Roro had been knowing Terri for years, and even though she got the shit beat out of her for talking shit, she never got her ass whooped for talking "about" shit. Therefore, Roro thought it would better to talk a little, but haul ass because Terri loved gossip, and she would hate to walk the dog on her ass in the middle of JANAF Shopping Center.

That wound up being a task for Roro. Every time she tried to leave, Terri brought up another conversation. "Okay girl, let me find these clothes and go," Roro said. Terri just followed her around the store to every rack, even picking out the same outfits as Roro.

Terri talked about everything, except what she really wanted to talk about, which was Dahlia. The only reason why she hadn't asked Roro about her yet was because she knew that Roro was game on and it would be hard as hell to get any information from her about Dahlia. She even knew that if she asked the wrong question, the wrong way, that Roro was going to cuss her ass out.

Terri was beginning to become tired of following Roro around the store and not getting any information, so she decided to come at Roro from a different angle.

"I have something for you to give to Dahlia." Terri reached in her purse and pulled out her wallet. "How is Dahlia by the way?"

"Bitch, she's good!" Roro said, refusing to comment on anything having to do with Dahlia. "So you're willing to pay me for some information on someone, that beat your ass? Either she beat a soft spot in your heart, or you're really the nosiest bitch in V A. Bitch which is it? Because you sending her money makes no fucking sense."

Terri didn't seem shocked by Roro's response, she damn near expected it. But what she didn't expect was her being so harsh.

"No!" Terri tried to explain and laugh it off. "Bitch your ass is crazy. But I really wanted to send her something, I just didn't know the address."

"Well she's good, and is not in need for shit... I'll let her know that she crossed your mind."

Sensing that Roro was irritated by the direction of the conversation, Terri told Roro she would call her later. "Girl let me help this nigga find something for these kids, before I have to fuck his ass up."

Finally Roro thought, relieved that she was finally leaving. "Yeah, do that." She continued to look through the racks of clothes, but this time in peace. *"Damn,"* Roro thought after she left. *"I should've took the damn money."*

***

Terri did call a few times after running into Roro at the store, but Roro kept the conversations short. She always pretended that she had something to do or that her mother had to use the phone. Roro thought of every excuse she could think of until Terri finally got the picture and eventually she stopped calling.

Roro felt like talking to Terri took up too much time. Terri already knew that she couldn't ask her about Dahlia, but that didn't stop her from talking about everyone else. Roro didn't have time for that bullshit. Roro wondered how in the hell Terri had the time to gossip on the phone with four kids starting school tomorrow, because she was struggling trying to prepare two kids.

The day before school started was draining for Roro. She was starting to realize that sometimes procrastination was a bitch and she would be better prepared next year. She walked over to her cousin's house, smoked a blunt and went back home to prepare for the boys' first day of school.

This day would be one for the history books, at least that's how Roro and Dahlia felt. It was Jeremiah's and Mecca's first day of kindergarten. Mrs. Pat and Roro helped Dahlia's parents out as much as they could, and by them working throughout the week, Mrs. Pat was responsible for putting Jeremiah on and off the school bus. Roro and Dahlia both loved that idea. They felt in a way that Jeremiah and Mecca were brothers and wanted them to always be together. They already had a bond. Unlike Roro and Dahlia, Jeremiah and Mecca's bond was before birth. They absolutely loved each other, so Roro and Dahlia didn't have to play a part in forcing them to get along. They understood already, it was as if some hidden forces of energy had them connected.

Roro took a shit load of pictures before she put them on the bus, and was prepared to take even more once school was over. She couldn't wait to hear what Dahlia had to say once she saw them, being that they didn't want Mecca to see Dahlia in jail. This way she could still witness his first day, even if it was only through pictures. Dahlia talked to Mecca on the phone every day, but now through the pictures, she could see firsthand just how big Mecca and Jeremiah were actually getting.

Roro looked at Jason sitting on the hood of his car across the street from the bus stop. She laughed on the inside, thinking about how funny it was that after she had to fuck his little girlfriend up, him and her were both quiet now. She thought it was even more hilarious because of the simple fact that the bitch had so much to say beforehand. *"Now that bitch only shows her face when she doesn't have a choice. I guess today it wasn't necessary,"* Roro concluded to herself.

Jason and Roro hated dealing with each other about anything, including Jeremiah. Mrs. Pat intervened and was now the one who dealt with Jason concerning Jeremiah. Roro didn't like it because she felt that Jason could get away with more by dealing with Mrs. Pat because of her kind spirit. That irritated Roro more than anything, and she never hesitated to let her know. Not only with Jason but anybody.

Everyone confided in Mrs. Pat about their problems and she loved it. Mrs. Pat was far from gullible but had empathy towards people and their different situations. People sensed that, and it drew them toward her.

When the bus arrived, Jason walked to the bus stop. "Hey. How are you doing?" he asked Roro, focusing on the bus.

She didn't acknowledge him, they had absolutely nothing to talk about. When the bus arrived, all of the kids rushed off the bus.

"You look handsome young man," Jason said to Jeremiah, looking at his first day of school outfit. He looked at Mecca, "Hey Mecca. What's up? You and Jeremiah are looking good bro."

Roro hugged Jeremiah and Mecca, then asked them about their day. She didn't say anything to Jason, just grabbed Mecca's hand and walked home. She didn't have to be around for Jeremiah to spend time with his father, so she left. She didn't want Jason anywhere near her. She never forgot what happened at the club that night. She hated that nigga, and if it wasn't for Jeremiah, he'd be dead. Even though she still thought about it, she never acted on it. *"He's lucky, and he doesn't even realize it,"* she thought as she prepared a snack for the kids.

Roro heard Jason in the front of the house, blowing his horn. *"I know that motherfucker don't think I'm going to the door. He can walk his stupid ass to the door like everybody else, fuck him. That idiot thinks he's privileged. Rude awakening fucker! You're in my domain now, and you're waiting on me. Yeah, keep waiting on it bitch!"* She laughed on the inside, continuing to slice apples to go with the kids snacks, now extra slow.

"Oh, that's Jason!" Mrs. Pat said rushing to the door. "You didn't hear him blowing the horn." Roro didn't answer. Instead she was upset at how her mother felt the need to run to the door. *"That nigga has legs,"* she thought.

Mrs. Pat came back in the house as quickly as she left out. "You can put Jeremiah's snack up for later," Mrs. Pat said to Roro.

"Why?" she asked Mrs. Pat, already knowing the answer.

"Child!" Mrs. Pat started off saying, trying to restrain her temper. "He's going with his father for a few hours." Roro burned with rage.

"Ma, it was his first day of school, I wanted to spend this time with him and Mecca. Who do this dude think he is yo!" Roro yelled as she placed Mecca at the table. "He could've picked him up tomorrow. I should've known when I saw his crusty ass outside that it was attached to some bullshit."

Mrs. Pat listened to Roro go back and forth, arguing with herself about Jason taking Jeremiah. Mrs. Pat didn't say anything, just let her vent... until she heard Roro curse. "Watch your mouth," she demanded. "Jeremiah is with his mother every day. Who are you to take his father from him? Whatever you and Jason got going on, that's y'all mess. But I can tell you this right now. He's only five years old and can't speak for himself. But me, I can and am going to speak for him, being that his parents are not capable."

Mrs. Pat didn't say anything else. She looked at Roro waiting on a response. After realizing that Roro didn't have one, she went inside her bedroom and continued reading her bible.

Although Roro understood and took into consideration what her mother said, her mother didn't know that Jason had put his hands on her, behind another bitch. For that reason alone, Roro could never respect him. Mrs. Pat would always have to be the mediator until Jeremiah was an adult himself. She now considered Jason an enemy. That was never going to change; she would hate him for the rest of her life.

CHAPTER 15

Snow Flurries

Roro ran from her cousin's house to the bus stop. It was easier for her to make it to the bus now that Jeremiah and Mecca were in school. She could literally wait until the last minute, then run as fast as she wanted, without dragging anyone behind her. *"Just in time,"* she thought, seeing the bus in a distance. She only had a few clients that day, and she was okay with that. Besides, she promised Mecca that she would take him and Jeremiah to the park after school. She hadn't had time to do much of anything lately, seeing that she was always booked. So, spending what she considered down time with the boys, or her smoking a blunt, was A-OK with her.

Usually after Roro finished her clients, she would wait around to see if anyone else might pop up without an appointment, but not today. She was headstrong on her date at the park with her boys and nothing was going to stop that. She took off her smock and threw it in the hamper at her job then walked to her station and started putting her tools up.

"Roro, you have a request," she heard the receptionist say.

"I'm leaving," she responded, not bothering to look up and see who the unexpected client was.

"What time do you close?" Roro heard the client ask. "I thought she would be here until 4...so I came all the way from Carolina for nothing, who's gonna pay for my gas?" Roro ignored the lady, deciding not to pay that shit any mind.

After Roro finished putting her tools away, she walked toward the front door. She not only heard the lady's anger, she could also feel her negative energy when she was about to leave out the door.

"That bitch shouldn't be doing hair if she really don't want to. This shit ain't for everyone," the lady said to the receptionist, making sure it was loud enough for Roro and anyone else to hear.

Roro without hesitation, sat her hair bag on a chair in the waiting area and walked over to the client.

"Did you make an appointment?" she asked.

"No, I didn't." The lady tried to respond again, but Roro cut her off in mid sentence.

"So there you go...you didn't make a fucking appointment. That's your fucking gas that you ran out, not mine. And what dumb ass motherfucker would drive all the way from Carolina without an appointment? My schedule is usually tight, so who's to say that you would've gotten your hair done by me anyway. And my mother didn't raise no bitches, BITCH!"

Roro turned around, grabbed her bag and stormed out of the salon. She didn't give the client a chance to say another word. Roro could tell that the lady was surprised at the way Roro came off, not even the receptionist expected it. Roro didn't give a fuck though. Although she loved her job, nobody was going to disrespect her, she didn't care who it was. Especially not by calling her a bitch. "This bitch got me all the way fucked up!" Roro said as she walked away from the salon, but looking at the door behind her, to see if the lady was brave enough to come outside. She didn't see her and continued to the bus.

After Roro got off the bus, she stopped at the 7-11 to grab a few bags of chips for the kids before she walked home. She proceeded to open the door, when she heard Jay's voice, "I got it." He reached his arm out and pushed the door open so she wouldn't have to touch it.

"Thanks," she said as she walked out the door, not wanting to turn around.

"That doesn't work with me," Jay said as he walked closely behind her.

"Okay, he opened the door, why can't he just let it be?" Roro thought to herself before turning around. She was forced to engage into some sort of conversation. She didn't know what on earth they could possibly have to talk

about, unless it revealed the whereabouts of his punk ass sister, or her friend, fake ass Gina.

"What's going on?" she asked annoyed.

Jay knew why Roro felt the way she did and felt like she had every right to feel that way. But he also could tell , that she wasn't all hard. She had a sweet side that she hid from the world. "Why are you trynna be so hard?" he asked, trying to make her feel more comfortable.

"Hard? Nigga I ain't trying to be hard...Look I gotta go, talk to you another time." She rolled her eyes and walked away. When Roro glanced back, she saw he still stood there, watching as she walked away.

"Look on bitch!" she mumbled before crossing the street. *"I don't get people yo."* She continued walking, getting closer to Red's friends that always stood in the same spot day in and day out.

"Yo...Yo!" they yelled at her.

"If you ain't got no money, then keep your comments to yourself," she said to herself, remembering a conversation

with one of her cousins, deciding not to give them her attention.

Later that day, when the boys got off the bus, Roro gave them their lunch and took them to the park, as promised. She noticed she was running behind Jeremiah the whole time and Mecca wasn't playing at all. She would catch him glancing at the sky every now and then, but no playing.

"Hey Mecca," Roro called to him. "Let's get on the sliding board." Mecca walked over to Roro, and held his arms out. When she picked him up, he laid his head on her shoulder. She knew that something was wrong but didn't know what.

"What's wrong Mecca?" she asked, rubbing her hand up and down his back.

"I can't find the Big Dipper," he said and started to cry.

"What do you mean, Mecca?" she asked. Mecca explained to Roro that him and his mommy would always come to the park to see the Big Dipper. He didn't know what he did wrong because his mommy wasn't here anymore, nor was the Big Dipper.

Roro's eyes filled with tears. She tried to hold them back, but she couldn't. She explained to him that the Big Dipper only came out at night and that he had nothing to do with his mommy not being here.

"She loves you more than anything. She just has something that she has to handle first, that's all. Trust me, if she could be here with you right now, she would. She hates that she's not able to hold you, that's why she calls you everyday," Roro assured.

"Come on Mecca," Jeremiah said. When Roro looked down, she saw Jeremiah holding his hand up toward Mecca. Roro put Mecca down and watched Jeremiah lead Mecca to a park bench. Jeremiah put his hand on Mecca's shoulder. She was happy to see them corresponding with one another, like two little men. She wondered what they were saying but didn't want to impose. Whatever was said worked because out of nowhere, they both jumped up and ran to the sliding board. It was like nothing had happened.

Roro couldn't believe her eyes, she was so proud of Jeremiah. She was raising him to be a strong man, but she never thought that it would start to show so young. She patted herself on the back as she sat on the bench, watching them do their thing.

She knew this day would forever be imbedded in her mind. Mainly because it was the first day that she realized that the boys bond was just as tight as her and Dahlia's. Now she just had to teach them how to protect themselves from the world. She would teach them that they were all they had and to protect each other.

Roro stayed at the park as long as she could, to find the Big Dipper for Mecca. She would explain to Mrs. Dot later after dropping him off, because she already knew that they had already come to pick him up. She couldn't remember where the Big Dipper was, so it was going to take her a while to find it. *"Shit,"* she thought, *"he's just going to have to spend the night."*

Roro sat on the bench and rolled herself a blunt. The kids are going to be tired as hell tonight; she smiled at the thought. *"Okay it's dark enough, let me try and find this big ass spoon,"* she thought as she looked up at the sky, seeing it filled with stars.

"Look, Mommy!" Jeremiah yelled. "I can see the Big Dipper! Mecca found it!"

Roro was relieved, but disappointed in herself. Relieved because she didn't think that she was going to be able to find the cluster of stars. But disappointed because she didn't understand how in the hell a five year old knew where it was and she was lost in the sauce. *"Damn, only Dahlia's son,"* she thought to herself before joining them. They marveled at the beauty of the sky for a few minutes longer and headed home.

After Roro explained everything to Mrs. Dot, they decided that it was best for Mecca to stay with her for the night. She bathed and fed them, then sent them in the room with Mrs. Pat.

"They should be sleep soon, Ma," she said searching for her shoes. "I know I just sat my shoes by the door." Roro thought of all the places that she would leave her shoes, it wasn't many. *"Damn, the house isn't that big,"* she thought but then remembered. "Jeremiah, where are my shoes?" she yelled.

"I don't know," he yelled back.

"If I don't find my shoes by the time I count to ten, I'm spanking butt."

Roro slowly counted to ten. *"What in the hell?"* she thought, realizing that Jerimiah wasn't going to budge. *"Damn, now I'm going to have to whip his ass."* Roro didn't want the day to end on a bad note because they had had a lot of fun with each other that day. She didn't want it to end with her giving out ass whippings. "Eight," she counted out loudly. Mrs. Pat's bedroom door slung open. *"Finally,"* she thought, hearing little feet running into the bathroom.

"Here you go, Aunt Roro," Mecca said, handing her the missing shoe.

"What?" she asked, surprised that it was Mecca and not Jeremiah bringing the shoe. "Who hid my shoes?"

Mecca didn't seem to have any time to answer that question. Whatever they had going on in Mrs. Pat's room was calling him so, he had to go.

"Thanks," she yelled, only to the door though because he had already slammed it behind him.

Roro didn't care who hid them, even though she had her suspicions. She had them, without having to whip any ass. Satisfied that she could continue being the good guy for the night, she walked across the street to her cousin's house.

June already had a blunt in rotation with a few of her friends before Roro got there.

"What's up Roro?" her friend Toni asked, happy to see her.

"What's up chick?" Roro responded equally as happy.

Roro sat down at the kitchen table and waited on her turn to hit the blunt. Roro didn't fuck with a lot of people, but

Toni was one of the real bitches. Whenever Roro got into some real beef, she was always down for whatever, no questions asked. They had a mutual respect for each other because when shit was reversed, it was always the same energy given.

"What's been up with you?" Toni asked.

"Girl, nothing really," Roro answered. "It's the same old shit, but a different day. I'm just tryna maintain out this cruel motherfucker for real, you feel me."

"Yeah, I feel you sis. It's the same shit here. Just tryna stay out the way and keep a leveled head. Yo, I heard about your girl, how's she doing?"

"Maaan," Roro said passing the blunt to June. "It's some bullshit going on. My girl is still down yo."

"Yeah, I heard, but she gonna be good though, right?"

"Yeah fam, she's gonna be good."

Roro had respect for Toni but wasn't in the mood to do too much talking on it. She was still in her feelings about what happened at the park with Mecca. Besides, they were all smoking. Jeremiah and Mecca had already blew her high from earlier. This was a sensitive topic, and it was a sure way to blow it again. All she wanted to do was relax her mind and chill.

Toni, feeling a vibe from Roro, changed the subject. She started telling them about this new bootleggers spot that everyone was hanging at.

"That's the new spot," Toni's friend informed. "Especially on week nights when you don't have shit else to do."

"You damn right," Toni intervened. "The spot is where it's at on the weekends, shit, fuck the club. You'll wound up in a jail cell fucking with the damn club."

"Amen to that," Roro agreed and held her hand up. "I can contest to that."

"Bitch please," June said. "The club ain't your enemy, Social Services is." Roro choked on the smoke she had just inhaled. June snatched the blunt from her hand. Roro was still coughing. "Yeah, let that smoke settle in for a few." June took a long puff.

"Shit where's this spot at?" June asked. "I mean…damn, if this is where the niggas at, I'm with it."

"A lot of niggas do be there too girl," Toni said. Toni explained that the house belonged to some older dude, but a Jamaican guy named Jay ran it. "And y'all," she said, "his ass is sexy as hell."

Roro and June looked at each other both surprised at hearing Jay's name. "Yeah, I've been to that spot once," Roro said. "I liked it but it's been a minute since I've been back though. Jay seems cool."

"Do he get money though?" June asked, cutting Roro off. No one in the room was surprised with June's question about money. Everyone knew that she chased the money bag, but she herself didn't work. Most of the men she dated were big time drug dealers. She never messed with the guys standing on the corner, she only gave time to their bosses. To her anything under that was just a waste of time.

"Oh, he got money," Toni's friend confirmed.

"Yeah," Toni agreed. "The brother ain't lacking in that department. And did I tell y'all that he was sexy as a motherfucker?"

Again June looked at Roro, this time raising her eyebrows. "Well, it sounds to me that whoever he gets with, is gonna be a lucky bitch, huh?" June asked, hinting to Roro that she better jump on it. "It couldn't be me."

Roro tried not to focus on that part of the conversation. She had other questions she wanted to know. "Don't he have a sister?" she asked Toni. "Where's that bitch at?"

"Okay bitch," Toni said, picking up on the animosity. "You know his sister?"

"Naw, not really," Roro said. "Only that she's Smoke's girlfriend."

"Oh, hold up!" Toni said. "That's the bitch that helped Smoke take little Mecca out of the country? A sneaky bitch!" Toni went on to tell Roro that she had seen Jay's sister a few times with some girl that she described to be

Gina. She also told Roro that she hadn't seen her in a while but still saw her friend every now and then.

"Whenever you see that bitch, let me know," Roro demanded. "I have to personally fuck that bitch up, no question. That bitch ain't no woman. She was on some bullshit, and I didn't trust her dusty ass from the start. I told Dahlia that the bitch was on some dumb shit. Fam, I could feel it. If you sit back and watch a snake, the bitch won't have any other choice but to reveal themselves."

"Oh, I got you," Toni agreed. "I most definitely will let you know the next time that bitch show up. See, that's that ignorant shit. You coming here, not knowing who knows who. That bitch didn't expect me and Dahlia to know each other. Every time I go there now, I'm going to make sure I'm ready for whatever. You know the count," she told Roro. "If your fists go up, so do mine."

Roro already knew that Toni had her back, but she wanted Gina to herself. "Thanks fam, but I got this one. Now if someone else jumps in, then by all means, do what you do, but that bitch...I have to get her because this is personal."

"I know that that's your spot," Roro said to Toni, "and I don't want to fuck that up. I, on the other hand, don't have a reason to hang over there. So for me, I can just whip her ass really good that night and be done with it, until I see her again. Every time I see her, Imma kick her ass and that's just what it is."

June understood where Roro was coming from, "You're damn right cousin, and if that guy with the money doesn't understand then trust me, it's another nigga out here with way more."

Everyone in the room looked at June. "You're a whole different type of bitch," Toni said to her, while Roro and her friend just shook their heads.

"What the fuck is wrong with y'all?" June asked. "It's a lot of men in these streets that like spending money on beautiful women. I'm not knocking the men that don't spend their money, I just find the ones that do, extra sexy."

"We feel ya," Toni said. "I fucks with ya however you roll, ain't much to that... However, Roro...back to the situation at hand. If I see that bitch over there, I'm most definitely calling you."

***

A few days later, Roro was finishing up Dahlia's client Jane's hair, before she got off from work on a Saturday night.

"How is Dahlia doing?" Jane asked.

"She's doing good...considering," Roro said.

"Yeah, I know."

Jane felt guilty that Dahlia was in prison. She felt like if she would have done more to get her out of that neighborhood, maybe none of this would of never happened. "It's partially my fault," she said and explained why she felt that way. "If only I could've convinced her to move out."

"It wasn't your fault," Roro said.

"Yeah, Dahlia really wanted to leave, but she wasn't financially stable at the time...and I knew that," Jane responded. "I've been coming to Dahlia since she was in hair school. I had an idea on what type of income she was working with. I just should've been more clear."

Jane turned around in the salon chair and looked Roro in the eyes. "Can you make me a promise?"

"I'll try my hardest," Roro responded.

"If I find somewhere for you to go, will you take me up on the offer?"

Roro, not hesitating said, "I sure will."

"Good," Jane responded, turning around in the chair, so Roro could finish her hair.

When Roro finished, her and Jane exchanged numbers, and she told her to tell Dahlia to call her. "Let her know that I'm here and that I'll never forget about her. Tell her to call me anytime, and I'll make sure, that I keep money on the phone for her."

"Okay Jane," Roro promised and leaned in to hug her. Jane got in her car and left.

Roro knew that Jane was serious about finding her somewhere else to live. She also knew Dahlia and understood that she wanted to do things on her own after being taken care of all of her life. There was no way that Dahlia was going to move anywhere if she herself couldn't afford it. Roro cleaned and packed up her tools. She was extra excited, because tomorrow was Sunday, and she could finally relax on her day off.

The next day Roro sat on her porch waiting for Mr. Chris to finish his Sunday drink alone, without sharing with his homeboys. This particular Sunday, instead of Mrs. Pat going to her usual early church service, she decided to go later that evening because a well known pastor was in town and would be speaking that night.

It was also a blessing in disguise for Mr. Chris. Usually when a pastor would visit the church from out of town, Mrs. Pat would get home late. That meant that he could drink at his own pace, in peace, and without feeling rushed.

As she waited on the porch, June ran out of her house and looked in her direction, yelling something that she couldn't hear. Roro walked to the end of her driveway to get a clearer understanding.

"The bitch is at Jay's house" she yelled.

Roro didn't respond. She immediately turned around and started walking toward the house. When Roro walked inside the house, she saw Mr. Chris sitting back in the chair enjoying his third forty ounce of Colt Forty Five. He looked so comfortable and she hated to burst his bubble but she'd been waiting to see this bitch for years, and now was her opportunity.

"Hey, Mr. Chris," Roro said, trying to think of a good enough reason as to why he had to leave. She had to be smart, so he wouldn't catch on. That would be hard because he knew that her mother would be at church for the majority of the night. "Something unexpected came up, and I have to leave. Just come by here a little earlier next Sunday, and I promise, I got you."

Mr. Chris was a little confused over the sudden change of schedule. He was in his feelings, but being that he did get to drink a few beers alone, he was okay with it. Besides, he would have a few hours longer next week to drink in private.

"Okay" he said, trying to catch his balance as he stood up. He wrapped the rest of his beer in a brown paper bag and walked out the door. "See you next week."

As soon as he walked out, Roro changed into a t-shirt, some sweat pants and tennis shoes. She also remembered how Dahlia grabbed Terri by her tracks so decided to put her hair up in a ponytail. *If that bitch grab my hair, I'm killing her ass,"* she said to herself. As soon as she finished, she walked across the street to June's house.

June was already in her car waiting for Roro. Not only was she ready to back her cousin up, but she was planning on finding her a new baller. That way she could kill two birds with one stone. Roro jumped in the front seat, and they headed to the bootleggers spot.

When they pulled up, Toni and three other girls were sitting outside in the car waiting.

"What's up?" Toni asked as she got out of the car, ready for a fight.

"Where the fuck this bitch at?" Roro asked, looking at Gina's car.

June popped open her trunk, grabbed her aluminum bat and walked towards Toni and Roro. "Where's this bitch at?" Let's go inside and wreck this shit."

Roro didn't want to handle it that way. She didn't really have any bad feelings towards Jay but wanted Gina bad, real bad. She grabbed the bat from June and walked over to Gina's car. "Imma make this bitch come outside," she yelled and smashed one of Gina's headlights out with the bat.

Some of the people outside gathered around, watching Roro demolish Gina's car, beating it with a bat, staring from the front and working her way toward the back. She beat out the windows, dented the body work...whatever was on the receiving end, was damaged. She didn't guide the bat, wherever it landed was fine with her. Every busted light, window and dent, was the damage that Gina caused Dahlia, Mecca, and Dahlia's parents when she plotted to take Mecca out of the country.

"Bring your ass outside bitch!" Roro yelled, still working her way around the car. "Where are you at bitch?" Roro prayed that Gina would come and save her car, looking up towards the house after each blow she landed. "Come on pussy! Where are you? I'm looking for you, now bring your ass!"

This time when Roro looked toward the house, she saw Gina looking out the window. That fueled Roro even more, so she started beating on the hood of her car. "When are you coming?" she yelled at the window.

Gina and two of her friends ran out the door, with Jay running close behind them. Roro threw the bat down and prepared to demolish the bitch, the same way she just did her car. But the closer Gina got, she saw the knife in her hand go up in the air.

Roro immediately blocked her face with her arm, causing Gina to slice her arm. Being that June was standing beside Roro, she side punched Gina, causing her to drop the knife. Roro knew that she was cut but her adrenaline was high—she knew then that she was going to kill the bitch.

She remembered being pulled off of Gina, and Gina was halfway in one of the windows she just smashed out. She wasn't finished yet, so Roro fought her way away from whoever it was holding her, to finish what she started.

As she continued punishing Gina, out of nowhere, she felt something hard hit against her skull. The blow was hard enough that it caused her to immediately stop fighting and grab ahold of her head. She could see June, Toni, and Toni's friends all fighting. She even saw Jay fighting some guy but didn't know why. Roro took her hands from her head, noticing that they were covered in blood and that was the last thing she remembered.

The next thing she could remember was someone holding something under her nose, to wake her up. Jay, Toni , June, and her friends all surrounded her. Roro tried to sit up, but her body felt too heavy. "Are you okay?" Jay asked, pushing her back down.

Roro didn't know how to handle Jay standing there, and as soon as she felt enough strength, she started swinging again, but this time at him. "Wait," Toni and June yelled at her, trying to explain his reason for being there, while he tried his hardest to hold her hands down.

When she was strong enough, she sat up and looked at the crowd to see if Gina was anywhere in sight. "Them bitches done got their asses kicked, and gone home," Toni said, knowing who Roro was looking for. Roro stood up, still wobbly, but with the help of Jay, and he walked her to June's car.

"I'm going to follow y'all to the hospital," he said when she got in the car. By now, Roro was now fully aware of what was going on around her.

"What hospital?" she asked. "I'm not going to nobody's fucking hospital. Either take me to them bitches house, or take me home."

"You're shitting me!" June said to Roro, already deciding without Roro's consent that she was going to the hospital. "With that blow that you received, how could I ever explain or face my Aunt, if you die in your sleep, or anything else? Bitch, we're going to the hospital," she said, telling Jay and one of his friends that it was okay to follow them.

Toni told June to keep her posted then told Roro that she'd talk to her tomorrow.

"Okay, thanks girl," Roro said.

"Anytime," Toni said and gave her a huge hug. "But please just go to the hospital to shut these bitches up," she whispered in Roro's ear.

On the way to the hospital, June told Roro that one of Gina's friends had hit her in the head with the bat.

"What bat?" Roro asked. "Do you mean your bat that you brought out there? How in the hell, did y'all bitches let them hit me in the head with a bat that you brought to a fight?"

"Bitch what?" June asked. "You took the motherfucker from me and threw the bitch to the ground like it wasn't shit. I mean damn, the way you did that shit, it seemed to me like your ass knew what you were doing. But now I know you don't."

"Fuck you," Roro said, trying not to laugh, noticing that when she did, it made her head hurt more.

June also explained how one of the guys there couldn't take the ass whipping that Gina was getting, so he attempted to hold Roro while Gina fought her. Even though Jay's intentions from the start was to break it up. When he saw the guy grab Roro, Jay reacted, causing him and the other guy both to go to their cars. Thank GOD they had mutual friends that stopped that before it escalated.

As Roro sat in the hospital waiting to be seen by a doctor, Jay and his friend Rich joked the entire time, which kept her and June laughing and made time fly by. Even though Roro explained that it made her head hurt more, they continued joking.

"See," Jay explained. "Fighting is for men, you're too pretty for that." This night in general made Roro look at him differently. She wondered if he was really one of the good guys, and if so, how much did he really know about his sister taking Mecca to Jamaica. *"I'll find out in due time,"* she said to herself.

After receiving five staples in her head and ten stitches in her arm. Roro was diagnosed with a concussion and sent home with a prescription. They also told her that she had to take a few weeks off from work, which she absolutely hated. June on the other hand found herself a baller, exchanging numbers with Jay's friend Rich. Telling Roro every chance she got, how much she adored his name. At least someone got what they wanted that night.

Roro looked at Jay different after that night. Her and June started spending more time with Jay and Rich. Even though she thought he was cool, she still wanted to know everything he knew about Mecca's abduction. Dahlia told her previously that Jay gave Rodney the information she needed to get Mecca back. Roro wanted to hear it straight from the horse's mouth. She could do that herself by observing his body language, facial expression and his tone of voice. She was now starting to see him too regularly not to say anything, so before things got too serious, she decided that today was the day that she would flat out ask him the questions she wanted answered so she could put her mind to rest.

After smoking a blunt and June's house, Roro and June waited for Jay and Rich to pick them up to go shopping at the mall. "I can't believe you waited this long to talk to Jay about that shit," June said. "Usually you would have been asked him, what's up with that?"

"I don't know," Roro explained. "He seems so chill, I wanted to try and feel him out first. I'm so use to motherfuckers revealing themselves, and he won't. I have to admit, I can't read this nigga to save my life."

"Well you don't need to put that shit off another day. Ask him what you need to know, put that shit out there. I'm going to bring my shit, just in case he wanna trip. Just do me a favor Cuz and wait until after we go shopping first," June said.

"Okay, I got you," Roro agreed.

When they pulled up, Roro and June were already standing outside. "Wait a minute, I forgot something," June said, not expecting to see them driving in separate cars. "Roro, come with me right quick."

June and Roro walked inside the house and June passed Roro the gun. "You know how to use this right?" she asked. "I can't see what's going on to help you while sitting in another car. Maybe we should all ride in one car?"

"Bitch fuck that," Roro said. "Don't we have the same cousins?" Roro snatched the gun from her. She reminded

June that their boy cousins taught both of them how to defend themselves, including how to use a gun, if necessary. They walked outside and both jumped inside separate cars.

After Roro and June finished shopping, they decided to eat at the food court in Lynn Heaven Mall. Roro didn't want to ask him in front of anyone, she decided to do it when they were by themselves. Even though she had questions, she could wait without ruining June and Rich's day. She couldn't read him enough to know how he was going to respond. Either way she was good after what June had given her. She would light his ass up if she had to.

When they left the mall, they decided to go back to Jay's bootleggers spot and have a few drinks. While driving toward the spot, they were in the car alone, they continued laughing and joking. From out of nowhere, Roro blurted out the question. "Why did your sister help Smoke take Mecca in the first place?"

Jay didn't act at all surprised that she asked him that question. He actually looked relieved.

"I knew that question was coming, I just didn't know when," he said. "Smoke had us all thinking that your friend's dad had a hit out on him, that's why she helped him."

That wasn't enough for Roro. She wasn't satisfied at all, and needed more than that. "I would go for that but I know that she was in the courtroom when the judge gave Dahlia custody of him. So she heard the judge tell him that, with her own ears. Did she tell you that?" Roro asked him.

"He told us all that before they went to court. He was starting to have Mecca more and told my sister that was the reason why. But yeah, you're right. She should've known something wasn't right. But you know now, more than majority of people, how far he's willing to go. That nigga ain't made right," Jay said.

Roro listened to Jay talk, remembering Dahlia telling her that Rodney said the same thing. She also remembered that at one point, Smoke did have Mecca at his house more than Dahlia did. She understood how they felt that way, but she still couldn't trust it.

Yes, she was grateful that Kim handed Mecca over to the Jamaican authorities, and yes, she let them know everything that she knew, concerning Smoke and his son. She could even go with the idea that, his sister was stupid enough to believe Smoke. Shit happens in life, and some people are more gullible than others. But aside from all of that, she could never forgive her for trying to hit them with her car.

Roro changed the subject, keeping her thoughts to herself. His sister tried to commit a vehicular homicide on Dahlia. She at least had to punch his sister in the face one, or two good times to make herself feel better. She kept quiet, listening to the music and thinking about Dahlia.

Roro and June always enjoyed themselves when they were with Jay and Rich. Jay shut the house down that day so they could all chill while him and Rich cooked.

While Roro and June sat in the living room talking about everything that they bought from the mall, they heard a knock on the door.

They were going to ignore it at first, but whoever it was, kept knocking like they weren't going to leave anytime soon. Roro and June both looked at each other undecided on what to do.

"Bitch, this is yo nigga's house...you better let him know that someone is knocking on his door," June said with a smirk on her face.

"He's not my damn man," Roro clapped back, standing up to go let Jay know that someone was knocking on his door. Roro finally heard the voice of the person behind the door. "I know you're here Jay," the girl said. "I can smell the food."

"It's Gina," Roro said to June. They both jumped up and ran to the door, deciding not to tell Jay and Rich shit!

Roro swung the door open, and Gina stood there shocked to see Roro opening Jay's door. Roro didn't want to ask any questions. Now was her chance to get her like she wanted. She immediately started throwing blows. She punched her for each stitch and staple she had to get on her body. She even gave her some punches for Kim not being there. Gina put up a little fight at the beginning but Roro seemed unfazed, and punched like a man. Roro was almost a professional at street fighting.

When Gina noticed June showing no signs of breaking them up, she decided that it was best to call out for Jay. June herself was mad as hell that her cousin got stabbed and hit in the head with a bat. So she did what she could to give Roro extra time to fuck Gina up a little longer.

"They can't hear you," June told Gina, pulling the door closed behind her. June, standing by the door, could hear Rich and Jay running toward the door so she tried holding it closed so that they couldn't get out. That didn't work, Rich slung the door open with very little problem at all, while Jay grabbed Roro.

"I'm going to get you bitch!" Gina yelled. "Y'all bitches jumped me."

"Wait, what?" June yelled, now feeling like punching Gina in the face herself. "I seen your kind before bitch. You can't accept the fact that you got your ass whooped, so you yell 'jumped'. Imma show you why I don't need no one, to fuck your ass up, you stupid ass hoe."

"Go home!" Jay yelled at Gina as him and Rich struggled harder to get Roro and June in the house. Wanting to get the last word, Gina kept yelling, telling Roro and June that they did jump her.

"Leave!" Jay screamed at her. After going back and forth a little, Gina eventually got in her car and peeled off.

Once she left, Roro and June walked in the house, with Roro feeling a little better. But June was furious. "That bitch is lying," she yelled at Rich as he walked her in the kitchen, trying to calm her down.

Jay looked at Roro not understanding how she could be so beautiful, but yet so wild. "Why do you act like that?" he asked, hoping that she could help him understand. "Can you see yourself? You're beautiful, why do you not care about all of these war wounds. Look at your arm, look at your head. You're a mom, right? How do you explain these type of actions to your son?" He paused to look at her softly, and continued. "Aren't you helping your sister out with her son while she's in prison? I don't get you yo." He shook his head and walked away, going inside of one of the rooms in the house, being sure to close the door behind him.

Roro sat down in the living room, staring at the scar on her arm. She could hear June and Rich in the kitchen going back and forth about her holding the door, trying to prevent them from getting out.

"What are y'all some kinda gangsters or something?" he asked June. "I mean is this how y'all were raised?" Roro laughed silently when hearing June tell Rich that she was raised to defend herself, and yes, she'd fuck a bitch up if necessary.

Roro didn't feel remorse for kicking Gina's ass, but she did feel bad for disrespecting Jay's house. She knocked on the room door to apologize.

"Come in!" he yelled.

This room looked totally different from the rest of the house. She didn't think that the rest of the house was dirty, but this room was immaculate. She looked at him as he laid on the waterbed, seemingly in deep thought.

"I'm sorry for disrespecting your house," Roro said.

"This isn't my house, but thanks though," he responded. "What about apologizing to yourself? I mean, I'm no one to you, you barely even know me, but you know everything about yourself. You just got stitches out of your arm yo. Look at your arm," he demanded. "That's something that you and your husband are going to have to look at for the rest of y'all life. You have to live with that. You just got staples, taking out of your head! Your head yo, you're not even fully healed from a head injury, and you're already out here wanting to rumble in the jungle, I mean, what is this?" He paused.

"What if you were just hit in your head again, same spot, then what? Who's going to raise your son, like you want him to be raised? He's watching you, his mother. Everything you do he's watching you. What if he comes home after a fight with stitches in his arm, or staples in his head...how would you feel? You never think about anyone else, not even your own mother yo."

Jay walked out the room, leaving Roro standing in the middle of the bedroom floor thinking of all of the fighting and cussing that Mecca had witnessed from her throughout the years. It would be harder for him when he became her age, with him being a black male. She couldn't imagine herself having to witness him going back and forth to jail, stabbed or shot. She knew that she had to change, she just didn't know how.

CHAPTER 16

Snow Squalls

Three years had gone by since that life-changing conversation with Jay. Roro and Jay have been in a serious relationship since that day, three years ago. Mrs. Pat and the boys loved it. Mrs. Pat loved it a little more because she could see her daughter slowly changing. Although Roro changed, she couldn't change everything overnight. She still had a lot of work to do when it came to her anger.

Roro hadn't been in any fights lately, mainly because she really wasn't going out like she used to, being that she was always with Jay. And whenever she did go out with June, the people that they were usually around already knew not to cross her. Although she tried to overcome her demons, dealing with stupid bitches along with her anger was the hardest.

One Sunday afternoon Roro sat in the living room painting her nails. Mecca and Jeremiah asked if they could go to the park because they were tired of playing the game. Roro sometimes allowed them to go to the park by themselves, because it was fairly close to the house. "Yeah, but stick together," she told them before they left.

That seemed to be a very peaceful Sunday. She felt relaxed with Mrs. Pat away at church, and now the kids were at the park. What more could she ask for. Mr. Chris didn't even come over as he usually did, so now she could chill and do her own thing. Maybe after her nails dried she could even walk across the street to June's house and back before the kids came back home. Little did she know, her peace would be short lived. Something was brewing at the park, she just didn't know it yet.

***

It all started because of some fat boy around the age of 12, trying to bully them. The boy thought that he could intimidate them because of his size, not realizing that they were raised by a real female thug. And if Roro would've found out, the implications would've been way worse than what some fat boy could've done.

Once the boy realized that they weren't going to back down, he slapped Jeremiah in the face. Mainly because he had the most comebacks and wouldn't keep quiet. That was a grave mistake.

Jeremiah fought the oversized bully as hard as he could, but the boy was too big. Mecca knew that him and Jeremiah both were going to be no match, so he did like his Aunt Roro taught him. He quickly observed the area around him. On the other side of the fence, he spotted a broken bottle. He ran to the fence, climbing over it with ease, opting to leave the bottle for a large piece of shattered glass.

Once Jeremiah returned to the boy sitting on Jeremiah, punching him repeatedly, all Mecca could hear was Aunt Roro telling him and Mecca, "If you can't beat them, join them." So he decided to do just that. Mecca sliced the boy with the broken glass one good time in the middle of his back. The boy rolled over to his side, screaming as loud as he could. The yellow t-shirt that he was wearing started to show blood.

When Jeremiah stood up, he immediately started kicking the boy. He didn't know that the boy had been stabbed. He thought it was one of his amazing punches that knocked the boy over to his side.

Mecca just stood there, in disbelief that he had drawn blood from someone, thinking he was probably going to jail like his parents now. What was he going to do around all of those big men, he was too small. He had to think of something, and fast.

Jeremiah got off the ground, immediately looking at the older boy reaching towards his back, and saw blood. He immediately looked at Mecca with his eyes wide opened. That's when he saw Mecca standing there with broken glass in his hand. "Oh shit!" Jeremiah blurted out.

Mecca finally did come up with an idea. He dropped the knife and started running. Jeremiah stood there for a second, until finally coming to grips with what just happened, followed suit. He passed Mecca as they both ran home.

They were so happy that it was the weekend and Grandma Pat was at work. But they didn't know how they were going to tell Aunt Roro that they just killed someone.

"We can't say anything," Mecca instructed, wanting to come up with a plan, before they went inside.

"I know," Jeremiah agreed. "We have to act as normal as possible."

"Hey bros," Roro said as they quickly brushed by her.

"Hey!" they replied in unison, walking fast toward the room.

"What the fuck is wrong with them?" she mumbled to herself, wondering if they were acting weird, or if it was all in her head from the blunt she just smoked.

"Do you think she knew?" Jeremiah whispered, closing and locking the door behind him.

"How in the hell do I know? I'm just a kid... I can't read grownups minds," Mecca responded.

"What are we going to do now?" Jeremiah asked.

Mecca shrugged his shoulders, "I don't know, I have to think this through," he said, sitting down beside Jeremiah on the bed.

They looked at each other, when they heard someone banging on the front door. Jeremiah jumped up and cracked the door, so he could try to see who it was. Hopefully he would be able to hear a little better. He looked through the cracked door and saw his mother walking towards the door.

"Who the fuck is it?" she yelled before opening it. She was highly upset by the way they banged on the door instead of knocking. She flung the door opened.

"What's going on?" Mecca asked impatiently.

"Wait a minute!" Jeremiah said. "I can't see shit!"

"Jeremiah and Mecca!" Roro yelled. "Get y'all scrawny asses out here, right now!"

"Oh shit!" Mecca blurted out, "…is the police out there?"

Thinking they were on their way to jail, they hesitantly walked toward her as slow as possible.

"Come on," she commanded. "And hurry y'all asses up!"

She startled them, forcing them to damn near run toward her. When they were close enough to hear what she was saying, she whispered to them, "I knew y'all were on some sneaky ass shit." She rolled her eyes.

Mecca whispered back to her, "Aunt Roro, don't worry. I'll take the blame this time, so you won't have to go to jail."

"Go to jail?" Roro asked confused. Roro opened the door wide enough, so everyone could see each other face to face. Jeremiah and Mecca both looked at each other, happy to see the boy alive. And more than anything, they were relieved that there were no police in sight.

"Now what happened?" Roro asked them, waiting to hear a response. They both immediately started talking at the same time, trying to explain what happened.

"One at a time please!" she said.

Mecca nudged Jeremiah with his shoulder, hinting for him to speak up first. Jeremiah told Roro what happened from the beginning to the end. After Jeremiah told Dahlia how him and the older boy started fighting, Mecca admitted to seeing the broken glass and stabbing the boy in his back.

Roro turned towards the boy, checking out his size and how big he was compared to her boys. "I'm most definitely going to have a talk with them," Roro assured the lady, before attempting to close the door. The boy's mother wanted Roro to do more than just talking with them. She was already angered that her boy had a small cut on his back and now even more after finding out that it was from a broken piece of dirty ass glass found on the side of the street.

"Have a talk with them?" she yelled at Roro. "Your son was getting his ass beat, and your other son couldn't handle it...That's why his bad ass stabbed my baby in his back! What in the fuck are you raising criminals?"

"Okay now, you're gonna have to tone it down," Roro said, now deciding to step out onto the porch to join the lady and her son. "What you want validation on every word I say to my boys behind closed doors? Well you ain't gonna get it. As a matter of fact, carry your ass."

The boys mother was clearly unsatisfied with Roro's approach about the situation, causing her to become louder and belligerent, even saying that Mecca and Jeremiah were destined for jail.

"Jail!" Roro yelled. "Listen bitch...You want me to believe that these two little boys was bullying on your oversized son, as big as he is! Get the fuck out of here with that! How old is he anyway? I do know this...he's too fucking old to be fighting on an eight year old. He's the motherfucker you need to be worrying about going to jail. You're just as dumb as he is, coming over here showing me a fucking scratch. Now his ass will know the next time not to judge a book by its cover. Now get the fuck off my porch and carry your ass before I do something to you."

The lady was mad as hell. "Okay bitch!" she yelled before hurling up a loogie and spitting it in her face.

"Bitch no you didn't!" Roro yelled and punched the lady in her mouth. Roro turned around and walked away, wiping the spit from her cheek. Feeling the spit on her face caused Roro to snap. It seemed as though an unseen force had her turn back around and whip that lady's ass. The ladies son tried but was unable to pull Roro off of his mother, so he ran home and called the police.

Roro continuously beat the lady, even after hearing the police sirens. She didn't give a fuck who was out there, that bitch had to pay. Every time she thought about what the lady did, she became stronger. A few police officers grabbed Roro and put her in handcuffs in the back of the police car. Mr. Chris saw what was going on and rushed in the yard, making Mecca and Jeremiah go inside the house while he talked with the officers.

As soon as the boys got in the house, they ran to the window, crying at seeing Roro in the back of the police car. Mecca felt like all the grown-ups that he loved were going to jail, and this was the second time that he had something to do with it.

"Why am I here?" he cried out. "Why was I even born?"

Jeremiah stopped crying, and looked at Mecca. Everything that his grandma Mrs. Pat taught him came into play. "You were born because GOD wanted you here!" he said. "You're able to weather any storm. In fact no storm is greater than you. Better yet, you are the storm." Since that moment, Jeremiah started calling him Storm.

What they didn't notice in the midst of them crying and talking, was that the police had let Roro go because the boys mother didn't want to press charges, being that she spit in Roro's face. So, Roro and Mr. Chris were standing behind them listening to everything they said.

Roro couldn't take it anymore. Even though she was happy with hearing the way Jeremiah handled the situation at such a young age, hearing what Mecca was going through on the inside, broke her heart. She knew that he was hurting, but for the first time, she heard it from the horse's mouth.

That was when she realized that she couldn't let them see her in that predicament ever again. She had no other choice but to change. Roro tried to think about different ways she could of avoided the situation, like her mother always told her to do when she was younger. She thought about what caused her to fight the lady in the first place. *"Naw fuck that shit, that bitch spit in my face, Imma fuck her up when I see her again."*

CHAPTER 17

A Blizzard

Roro laid across the bed looking through Jay's photo album. She came across an old picture of Red and Kim.

"Wow!" she blurted out, amazed at seeing Red in the picture. Their friendship went way back, and they basically grew up together. It was almost identical to the way her and Dahlia's friendship was. She knew that they had been friends forever, but seeing it in a picture was totally different.

Jay laid behind Roro, watching as she flipped through the pages of his photo book. He noticed that she paused once she came across the picture of his sister and Red.

"I think they were in the 7th grade in this picture," he said, staring at the picture deep in thought. "I remember this day like it was yesterday."

Jay and Roro shared a lot of things with each other. She understood that even though Red and his sister weren't together anymore, they still had mountains of memories from childhood. So the thought of his friend doing a minimum 17 year bid, really fucked with his mental. Roro rubbed his hand that draped her waist slowly as they continued staring at the picture.

Jay never explained to Roro why Red was doing time for murder and she never told him that she already knew. She understood his feelings. As far as she was concerned, the feeling was mutual because she also kept Dahlia's personal life private. She knew that he had just as much information on Dahlia's case that she did, but neither of them brought it up. They only talked about Dahlia and Red finishing their bids, and that Dahlia would be home soon. Other than that, she didn't feel that Dahlia's situation concerned him. Yes, he was a good guy, but he was also Kim's brother.

One of the things that Roro respected about Jay was the fact that he was a realest. He didn't care who you were, if you were wrong, then that's what it was. Momma, daddy, sister, brother, or even Roro, he didn't care. She admired how him and Rodney were able to pick up the pieces after him and Kim split. He acknowledged that his sister was wrong and that was that. To Roro, that proved how much of a real man he was, and she loved that about him.

Roro continued looking from one page to the other when she came across a picture of him and Kim. Kim looked like she was around 8 or 9, and Jay had to have been around 5 or 6. "How cute," she said, placing her hand over her mouth laughing at Jay and Kim sitting on Santa's lap.

"Oh, you think it's funny huh?" Jay asked, snatching the photo album from her hands and closing it.

"No, I don't think it's funny," she answered. "I actually think it's cute! I mean, your teeth may be a little big but that don't mean nothing, you're still cute." She burst into laughter again.

"Ha! Ha! Ha!" Jay said sarcastically, putting the album on a shelf near his bed.

He laid back down behind her. "Are you okay?" Roro asked, reaching her arm behind her so she could rub his cheek.

"Yeah, I'm good," he responded, thinking of a way to change the subject. "Did you talk to Jeremiah today?" He rested his head on hers.

"No!" she said sharply. "I told you that he was at his father's house and you already know that I don't fuck with that pussy ass nigga."

Roro told Jay everything that happened years back at the club. He understood why she was angry, but he also felt like they needed some type of communication, other than Mrs. Pat.

"Look," he said, "Someone's gonna have to be the bigger person yo. I know that he shouldn't of put his hands on you, but the nigga can't do it now. One of us is going to have to be stable minded, and I suggest that it be you."

Roro sat up on the bed and turned around to face Jay. This nigga must be going crazy, she was thinking, confused with his last comment.

"Let me wear the pants, and you continue to wear the sundresses," he said, grinning at the facial expression that she was displaying. "I know he's a bitch ass nigga…but me being in a relationship with you makes it harder for me to look at that clown. Jeremiah is my little man, and you know that. But at the same time, I wanna kill his dad. You feel me?" Jay asked, hoping that Roro understood where he was coming from.

Roro laid back down on the bed, still facing Jay, ignoring his latest question.

"Feel me?" he asked again, wanting to make sure that they were on the same page.

"I hear you," she finally answered. But in reality, what she was really thinking was that it'll be a cold day in hell before she ever forgave Jason, let alone be on speaking terms with his dumb ass...fuck that nigga!

Roro and Jay wanted to get out and get some fresh air, so they decided to ride out and see what was going on around town. Usually they would hangout at the spot, but Jay didn't want to deal with it anymore. He felt as though it was starting to become hot. Once the younger crowd found out about it, he didn't want to deal with the headache. Now some younger dude was running it. Jay would pop up every now and then just to talk to the owner of the house, but he never stayed too long. It was always an in and out type of thing.

"Let's go over June's house," Jay recommended. "Rich is over there, let's see what they're talking about."

Roro laughed at the thought of Rich being at June's house. "So Rich is back over there?" Roro wasn't at all surprised, she just thought it was hilarious. Jay didn't laugh but looked at Roro and grinned because he knew why she laughed. He thought it was funny that she allowed Rich to come back over, after what happened the last time they were together.

Rich and June weren't officially a couple, only seeing each other every now and then or whenever it was convenient. A couple of months ago when Rich was at June's house, he accused her of getting him drunk and stealing money out of his pockets once he fell asleep. She never told Jay, but she knew that it was true because June bragged to her and Toni about it the next day. June was only being June, and that was nothing new to her and Toni, it was only new to Rich and Jay. She had been stealing his money the whole time and he finally noticed it that one time.

When they got to June's house, Jay and Rich ordered Chinese food. They had a few drinks, smoked some weed and sat around laughing and joking. It was a chill, calm type of night and everyone seemed to be in good spirits. Rich and June even acted like an actual couple, even if it was only for that night.

The alcohol started to run right through Roro, forcing her to run back and forth to the restroom. On her last trip to the restroom, she noticed that the toilet wouldn't flush. *"What the hell?"* she mumbled to herself. She started to call out to June, but halted after hearing someone walking through the leaves outside the window. Roro peeked out the blinds, and saw a police motioning to the other officers where to go as they quickly surrounded June's house.

Roro rushed out the bathroom, to warn everyone. Before she could utter one word, the police burst in the door, and forced them all to the ground. While laying on the floor on their stomachs, Roro couldn't help but think of how cool they were with just them two, chilling at Jay's house. That's where they should've stayed, instead of being surrounded by fifteen to twenty Norfolk police officers.

After being searched, the handcuffs were taken off. A plain clothes detective handed June a warrant while other officers went in and out of different rooms searching for something. "I found something!" one of the officers yelled. All of the officers, asides for a few, rushed inside of June's room to see what was found.

Hearing one of the the officer's reveal that he found something frightened Roro as she watched them all crowd inside June's bedroom. Roro, Jay and Rich all looked at June wondering what the police could've found. June was unbothered, more upset that they had ruined her night than about them finding anything.

"What?" June said irritated by both, them looking at her and the heavy police presence in her home.

After they finished searching June's room, one of the officers finally revealed to June that they found a 9 millimeter handgun and had reason to believe it had been used in a crime.

"We have to take it, so we can run it through ballistics. If that is not the gun that we're looking for, you can retrieve it after it has been tested," the detective said.

June didn't understand why they needed her gun. The only chance she had to use it was at the gun range. And that was only a few times. To her this was all bullshit. She felt as though they used her gun to justify a reason to kick her door in.

"That's my shit!" she yelled at the detectives. "You can't just come in my house and take a gun that's legally registered to me!"

"We'll be contacting you soon," the detective said. "I suggest you read the warrant."

"Fuck you!" June yelled at the officers, feeling as though it was another reason for their certain interest in her gun. "Fuck every last one of y'all." As the last one left, she closed the door behind them.

They tried to come up with any guesses on why detectives were interested in her gun. They all sat around talking about the situation when they noticed that Rich was extremely quiet.

"Why the fuck are you so quiet?" June asked, skeptical of his sudden silence.

"I used your gun," Rich mumbled under his breath, hoping that she didn't hear him. June wanted him repeat what she thought she heard him say because she couldn't have heard him right. She was under a lot of stress after what she just witnessed, so she was hoping that her hearing was off.

"What did you say?" June asked.

"I used your gun," he repeated. Everyone was speechless and Jay and Roro couldn't take their eyes off of him, hoping that he had some sort of a good explanation to why he would have to use her gun, and not his.

June didn't care why. She left out the room like nothing happened.

"Why would you use her gun man?" Jay asked confused.

"Man , you know how these niggas are in the streets. They already feel a certain way about us coming here interfering with their money. It's an all out war between

Jamaican and American street busters. I had to keep a gun on me and I felt more comfortable using hers, because it was legal. If I had of been stopped with hers it wouldn't have been as bad."

June returned to the room while Rich continued explaining the reason he used her gun without her knowledge. June walked behind him, plunging a pocket knife into his back. Jay and Roro were able to get the knife out of June's hands before she was able to do more damage than what she had already done. She didn't yell, fuss or fight, she just grabbed her pack of Newport's and chain smoked as many as she could, knowing that it would be a long time before she would be able to pull on one of them again.

The police were called back to June's house once again. This time they took June to jail, and the ambulance took Rich to the hospital. Even though he finally admitted to the authorities that he used the gun without her permission. The state gave her a more lenient sentence.

CHAPTER 18

An Avalanche

Roro and Jeremiah sat outside of Dahlia's parents' house, waiting on them to come home. Roro was now living in South Carolina, and drove seven hours for this day. Roro's heart started pounding, as she watched their car pull in the driveway from her rear view mirror. She jumped out of her car before they could park. Jeremiah was equally as excited, jumping out of the backseat, right behind her. She raced to their car, unable to wait any longer. On her way toward the car, she saw a woman with two braids in her hair get out of the back seat with Mecca, looking in her direction.

Roro couldn't believe it. Her sister and best friend was finally home at last. They cried tears of both joy and sadness as they hugged each other. The tears of joy were because Dahlia had made it home safely after doing eight out of a ten years sentence in prison. The sadness was because Dahlia had missed out on a lot, especially when it came to Mecca. She had a lot of catching up to do.

Dahlia looked at Jeremiah, unable to believe how much older he and Mecca looked since she last seen them. She didn't see them as much as she did Roro and her parents, by her choice. She preferred to talk to them more on the phone because she didn't want them to become too familiar with seeing people that they loved in prison.

After they talked for a few minutes, they all decided to walk to Roro's car. Roro opened the door to the backseat, revealing to Dahlia, the most beautiful baby girl that she'd ever seen.

"I can't believe that you're married with a baby," Dahlia said to Roro.

"Me neither," Roro said. Dahlia grabbed her sleeping GODdaughter, Nandi, out of the car seat and held her for the first time and walked inside the house.

Dahlia listened to everyone talk, trying to explain how things had changed since she was away. She was amazed at how technology advanced throughout the years, allowing her to walk around with her own personal phone. Roro talked to Dahlia and her parents for hours before deciding that it was time for her and Jeremiah to leave so that Dahlia could spend quality time with her family. Roro vowed to pick her up the next day.

The next day, Roro couldn't wait to pick Dahlia up. She wanted to show Dahlia how much Norfolk had changed since she'd been away. After riding around a bit, they ended up at the Virginia Beach Ocean Front. They watched the seagulls flock over the water in search for fish. The energy of calmness surrounded them, while the smell of saltwater filled the air. One thing didn't change for sure. Something about the oceanfront was soothing to the soul.

Roro and Dahlia started talking about some things that they didn't feel comfortable talking about during family visits or over the phone. Dahlia told Roro how some girls tried to take her kindness for weakness in prison, and how she had to handle that situation swiftly.

"What happened?" Roro asked.

"Girl it was behind that funky ass phone. Them bitches got certain people to control the phones in there and they want you to ask them for permission to use them. Well, I'm not asking a motherfucker for shit. I took it as they put them in there for us to use, so that's what I did." Dahlia paused briefly and continued.

"One day, I called Mecca. Well, one of them bitches felt some kind of way and hung up the phone on my baby. I didn't do anything at that time because her homegirls were standing around, but I knew that I couldn't let it slide because they would prey on that. The next day I wrapped a bar of that hard ass soap that they use in prison, inside of a pillow case. I waited until I saw that bitch by herself and beat blood from her ass. I had a few run ins after that, but they were small…nothing serious. Everyone knew not to fuck with me after that. I just kept to myself and only dealt with a few people. The people that I dealt with though were like me, so her friends surely didn't want any problems." Dahlia smirked. "But y'all…I missed y'all so much. I was more worried about you out here than I was about me in there. Thank you to the Devine for sending you Jay, he's a good balance for you."

"He's good for me. I'm still amazed at how he's able to get inside my head and make me understand things that I've been confused about for years. I had no choice but to marry him, I couldn't let Gina get him," Roro responded, and her and Dahlia both laughed.

"Girl he probably wouldn't want her dusty ass!" Dahlia responded.

"I know he wouldn't, I just had to get a laugh out of you," Roro said.

"Well you got it bitch. What happened to her by the way? Is she still in Virginia?"

"Naw, the bitch moved back to Jamaica. Her and Kim stupid ass look better there anyways."

"I can't believe that Kim is your sister-in-law," Dahlia replied.

"Yeah, the bitch is so called family, but she also know to stay in her lane. Jay has a relationship with her, not me. Fuck that ho!"

Dahlia got off the railing, opting for a seat on a nearby bench. Dahlia looked at Roro, with Roro already knowing what she was going to ask. "How did Mecca handle all of this, from your perspective?"

Roro sat on the bench beside Dahlia, ready to engage in more questions that she had held back for years. "He blamed himself a lot for you and Smoke not being around. I feel that he needed to place the blame on someone, so he put it on himself." Roro paused.

"I first noticed it that day that I had to whip that bitch's ass for spitting in my face," Roro reminded Dahlia. "Well, after the police released me, I overheard Mecca crying and talking to Jeremiah saying how both of his parents were locked up. Then girl...he questioned his life. That broke my heart," Roro said tearing up. "He thought that I was going to jail, so he started blaming himself. It was hard to see an eight-year-old putting so much blame on himself. That was just too much weight for someone his age to be carrying around."

"Most definitely," Dahlia agreed, looking away from Roro and looking at the waves of the ocean.

Roro went even deeper, telling her friend that she didn't know how bad it affected Mecca because he never talked about it. But her parents made sure that he stayed in therapy. "I offered to talk to him about it, but he never wanted to. She paused and hesitantly changed the subject.

"What happened that night?" Roro asked Dahlia, finally able to hear the whole truth.

Dahlia explained everything that happened that awful night. "I usually kept the gun on a shelf in my closet. But by me being home alone, and without Mecca being at my parents' house that night, I decided to put it in the drawer beside my bed. I felt more safe because by this point, my nightmares were getting worse." She paused, took a deep breath and continued.

"Smoke had gotten himself a key made and was going back and forth from my house, all without me even knowing. That made everyone else , from the outside, think that me and him were still an item, or at least having sex. So when he unlocked the door and came in that night, no one thought twice about it. I was the only one in the dark about it all. That night, I was in my bed sleeping and from out of nowhere, he just grabbed me by the neck and started choking me. I couldn't breathe, and thought that I was gonna die that night. I was finally able to kick him in his nuts, and make it to the drawer. I grabbed the gun, and then I shot him. Smoke really wanted me dead, I could tell. His adrenaline was extremely high because he was still trying to get to me, so I shot him again. I must've blacked out after that, because I don't remember but I did hear the gun go off, therefore I must've shot him once more." She looked at Roro, Roro had no comment, so Dahlia continued.

I had a hard time coping with his death right after everything. I still loved that man, and it hurt me to my soul that he made me do that to him. I questioned his feelings for me. Were they ever genuine, and what could I have done that made him hate me so much. We had more good memories than bad, so I thought, but evidently that wasn't so. The hard part is that I will never get an answer, and that hurts more than anything.

"I was in shock and couldn't move, everything was happening so fast. I knew that he was at my neighbors' house watching me the whole time, but for him to want me dead and not care that his son would no longer have a mother…hurt me more than anything. Who would've thought that me trying to save his life, by keeping him out of jail would later cause me to take his life and go to prison."

Tears ran down Roro's cheeks as she listened to everything Dahlia endured that night. Her best friend turned out to be stronger than she ever imagined .

After Roro dropped Dahlia off at her parents' house, Dahlia and her parents sat up and talked until 2 am. They had so much to talk about, and decided that they would continue in the morning because Dahlia was extremely tired. Dahlia had her own room, but opted to sleep with Mecca her first few nights home. She didn't care that he was now thirteen, he was still her baby and she missed him. She pushed him over, squeezing in to make enough room for herself and dozed off to sleep.

***

"What are you doing?" Dahlia asked Mecca, upset with having to see him in an orange jumpsuit. "Mecca, can you even begin to imagine the amount of shit that you're in right now?" She looked at Mecca's face from the other side of the video screen. This was the same infant that she brought home from the hospital. The same little boy that she watched grow over the years. Not the man society deemed as a thug.

Roro studied Jeremiah's body language while she tried to talk to him as he walked around in his room. She and him both knew that she was no stranger when it came to street life, and he never got that twisted. That's why it was certain things that he went out of his way to make sure that she didn't know. He knew his mother and didn't want to put her in any compromising situations. He rushed to leave the house because he knew that this one would be a hard pill for her to swallow.

"A storm had been here...unfortunately. But after the storm... you know, when the clouds dissipate, when there's no more thunder and lightning...no more rain...then what? What do you do after all of that? You process, you accept, and then you rebuild YOU! My name isn't Storm, it's Mecca."

Ice looked at Mecca, agreeing with everything he had just said to him. Ice then sat his gun on the kitchen table. "The Ice has melted... My name is Jeremiah."

***

"Ma!...Ma!...Momma! "Mecca called out to Dahlia, wanting her to wake up so he could fix her breakfast on her first week home. Dahlia grabbed him, holding him tight as she could. She told him about the dream she just had and made him promise to stay away from trouble.

"I promise, Ma," he said, rushing her to get dressed so that she could come eat.

"Okay son. I'll be in there, let me get myself together."

Dahlia picked up her cell phone, trying to figure out how to call Roro when all of a sudden, her phone started ringing. Still unaware of how to operate a cellphone, Dahlia eventually answered it, realizing it was Roro.

"You must've read my mind," she said into the phone. "I was just about to call you."

Dahlia started telling Roro about the dream she had last night, only to be cut off in the middle because Roro finished it by telling the same dream to Dahlia. They had done it again. They both had the same dream, at the same time, but this time it was concerning their boys.

"Yeah...but they're good boys," Dahlia reassured Roro. "They're not the type of boys that would get in any type of shit."

Dahlia and Roro both agreed that they had two magnificent young boys. They laughed at the thought of them getting in any type of trouble.

After hanging up, Dahlia got herself together and joined Mecca and her parents in the kitchen.

"Mmm, it smells good in here," Dahlia said to Mecca. Dahlia stared at Mecca while him and her father finished cooking breakfast for her and her mother. She watched the way he joked around with her parents. She looked at the way he innocently held his head to one side, while his grandfather showed him how to flip pancakes. *"Impossible,"* Dahlia told herself, smiling at him patiently waiting on his grandfather to tell him what to do next. *"That can't happen, he's a shining star, in a dark world...My boys ain't bout that life,"* she thought to herself. Dahlia thought about herself, and how she was before the world had changed her. *"Naw,"* she said, still convincing herself that it was just a dream.

After breakfast Dahlia and Mecca sat outside in the backyard, catching up on old times. "So what do you like to do?" she asked.

"Nothing much, I just play my game and chill with Ice...I mean Jeremiah," Mecca said, hoping that Dahlia didn't notice.

It was too late, she heard it loud and clear but wouldn't let him know. She had to play it cool, but the name Ice ran through her mind like a track star. She's been gone for a while, and she wanted him to feel comfortable talking to her.

"What?" she asked. "I never heard you call him that before. Where did he get that name?" she asked curiously.

"That's the name that our friends from school call him. Some of them live in Grandma Pat's neighborhood."

"How did they come up with that nickname?" she asked.

"People say that he is smooth as ice, so they gave him that nickname," Mecca explained.

"Oh, okay," Dahlia said, seemingly okay with Jeremiah's nickname.

"So Jeremiah's nickname is Ice...who are you?"

"Well Jeremiah calls me Storm...he's been calling me that since we were little, so now everyone else picked up on it. So, that's my name."

Dahlia wasn't upset with that because Roro had already hipped her about that. To her, Jeremiah had given him that name for uplifting reasons, and she actually thought that it was cool.

"Ma!" Jeremiah called, trying to get her undivided attention. "You have to promise me that when we're out you'll only call me Storm. Me and Jeremiah have a reputation to hold on too, and we can't do it with the names Mecca and Jeremiah."

Dahlia listened to Mecca talk and didn't say a word. She was mentally keeping notes. She'd been out of the loop for a while and had to learn quickly how to be two steps ahead of the both of them.

Later that night, when Dahlia's parents and Mecca went to bed, she sat in the backyard, stargazing. She couldn't believe how much older Mecca and Jeremiah had become. She thought that her parents along with Roro and Mrs. Pat had did an excellent job, and she was extremely grateful. She had missed out on a lot and had a lot to catch up on. But overall, they were two intelligent young boys.

She searched the sky, until she finally came across the Big Dipper and decided to keep her eyes placed there. *"How beautiful,"* she thought to herself, watching the universe and all it's magnificence. She loved the way The Universe was proving to the world, that even in total darkness, there would always be some form of light shining. *"Absolutely amazing,"* she thought. The best part was that she could sit outside for as long as she wanted, and no one could make her go inside.

"Oh shit!" Dahlia said out loud, as she jumped up, noticing a single star shoot across the sky. "Woah!" She closed her eyes, and made a wish, letting her wish escape her mind to join many others that also wished upon that same shooting star that night.

The last wish she made on a star was for something that she really wanted help with at that time. She didn't like the way she got what she wished for, but she loved receiving the gift at the end. She is now a firm believer of when you hear people say be careful what you wish for, some things are better left alone and without interference. If she had known then what she knew now, she would've just gone with the flow and let nature take its course. Every question that she had about Smoke, Rodney, and herself was answered, whether she liked it or not. She didn't like the process on how she was given her information, but she did love the gift afterwards.

This time, she wanted to be extra careful with how she made her wish, especially when it involved teenagers. She wished that Mecca and Jeremiah would grow up to be successful young men, despite the odds that were stacked against them. It was a cruel world, and she wanted them to depend on no one but themselves.

"That doesn't seem too much to ask for," she told herself after making her only wish. They are not bad boys, she probably didn't have anything to worry about. Dahlia started thinking of how she was before the world had changed her. No matter how much she hid things from her loved ones, or went against the grain with anything, it always felt good when she learned it on her own. Is that what her boys are going to have to go through. Could it be at all possible that Mecca and Jeremiah would soon go through their own journey and have their own story to tell? *"Naw, not my boys,"* she thought. *"That was all just a really bad dream."* She quickly remembered the name Ice being called in the dream. *"That was just a coincidence."* Or was it ?...Only time would tell.

CHAPTER 19

An Ice Storm

Dahlia and Mecca had been living in South Carolina for six years now and Dahlia absolutely loved it. Mecca and Jeremiah on the other hand, were back and forth to Virginia, only using Carolina as their address but stayed in Virginia most of the time.

When Dahlia wasn't working, she was at Roro and Jay's house majority of the time. If she wasn't there, she was more than likely with her Goddaughter Nandi inside of a tent in the backyard. Nandi loved doing that because her and Aunt Dahlia were able to watch the stars and the many shapes.

One night, Dahlia was sitting in her back yard sipping on a glass of red wine as she listened to Roro talk on the phone about an incident that happened in the salon.

Dahlia thought it was funny listening to Roro talk about a stylist and a client that were about to come to blows in the parking lot of the salon.

"I know you can relate," Dahlia said, remembering plenty of times that Roro had been in that predicament. "You was quick to ask a bitch to come outside." Dahlia laughed, but was very proud of the changes she saw in Roro, and she let it be known every chance she got.

Roro returned the love. She always told Dahlia how proud she was that she came home from prison and jumped right into a career that she was extremely passionate about. "Astrology is right up your alley. You've been interested in stars ever since we were scrawny ass little girls," Roro reminded her. "I'm proud of you."

"Okay, well if you're so proud of me, then take my GOD baby outside, and show her the lunar eclipse. I told her that you were going to show her..." Dahlia said.

"Damn, I almost forgot. Thanks for reminding me," Roro said, upset that she had to do it but at the same time wondering how Nandi would've taken it if she had forgotten.

"Is it tonight?" Roro asked hesitating to get off the phone.

"Yes it's tonight, we have been discussing this for a couple of months now. I tell you what... if you fuck around and don't show her this event tonight, Imma make sure I tell her personally that I reminded you about it, and that you intentionally refused to show it to her."

"You're a dirty bitch," Roro said. She laughed and hung up the phone.

Roro and Nandi sat outside on the deck in her back yard, waiting on the lunar eclipse. Roro's cell phone started vibrating like crazy. She had already turned the volume down and vowed to ignore it so she could spend some quality time with her baby girl, but whoever this person was wasn't having it. They called back to back, so it had to have been important.

Roro grabbed the phone and saw her homegirl Toni's name on the screen. That was unusual. Whenever Toni called and Roro wouldn't answer, she would normally wait until Roro returned the call. Roro quickly answered the phone, afraid to know the reason for the obsessive phone calls.

"Hey bitch, is everything good?" Roro answered, pausing to hear what was so important that make her call so many times.

Toni didn't answer Roro's question, instead she got straight to the point. "Don't say anything, just listen, because I have to get everything out before my phone dies. Quiet as it's told, we all know that when June finally touched down from prison, she was game on. She was full steam ahead trying to get her money up, not giving a fuck who she crossed. She even dabbled with selling drugs every now and then." She paused briefly and continued.

"Everyone around here know her, and for that reason alone, people let her slide here and there with a lot of shit. I told her ass that she needed to chill out before she gets someone in some shit, but the bitch ain't wanna listen. Well she stole a lot of money from this guy named Sly that she was fucking with from D.C, and now he's looking for that ass. I mean that nigga is searching everywhere for her."

"So the word is that Storm was standing near your mom's house, and Sly pulled up. I guess he must've gotten a whiff that he was her family or something...anyway Sly started asking a lot of questions about June. Storm felt a certain type of way about this unknown dude asking questions about his family. We're all from the same hood and grew up together. We also have mad respect for each other. Everyone also has known Ice and Storm since they were babies, so ain't nobody trynna go there with them for real. Sly on the other hand knows no one, so he simply don't give a fuck." Toni took a deep breath.

"A few words were said between them, and before anyone knew it, bullets were flying. I know one thing though. They said that Storm wasn't trying to injure ole boy, but he literally wanted that nigga dead yo. No one got shot or anything, but Imma tell your ass this bitch...Storm and Ice are something serious. You know I'm in these streets, and I've been hearing about them boys for a while now. They know and trust me, because they look at me as family. They also know that I'm watching them, and from what I see...it's you and Roro on steroids bitch!"

Roro just listened. "Storm is the thinker of the two, he's gonna strategize and come up with all of the ideas. Ice on the other hand, is gonna put in that work. Roro, your boy don't give a fuck. Put it like this... they say, that if Ice were there when everything popped off, Sly wouldn't have had a fighting chance. They'll put in that work apart, but when the both of them are together... they gone handle it right then and there. Basically shit is gone get done. I've even heard niggas say that when you wanted something done, that they were the boys to talk to... Now about that part, I don't know for sure, but that's word on the street," Toni said.

Roro was a little shocked to hear the details about her boys, but she let Toni finish. "Everyone gives them the upmost respect, including all the O.G's that we know. The crazy thing about it is how low key they are when they're around family and friends, that shit is wild. If I wasn't in the streets, and only seen them around family. I most definitely wouldn't know anything that they were doing out here. But by me being out here, not much is gonna get past me. They know that whenever they see me around, I'm watching they asses. Shit, I don't know if that's good or bad, but I'm still gonna do it. I don't hide the fact that I got my eyes on them, and as a matter of fact...I got a few other people watching them too. Imma most definitely keep you posted on everything that's going on," Toni concluded. Toni promised to keep her in the loop on everything going on with her boys in the streets.

When they hung up, Roro immediately wanted to call Jeremiah, but something inside her said "DON'T!" He was a grown man now, in his twenties. Besides, he wouldn't listen to her. She knew this because she always talked to him and Mecca. Whenever she would try to kick them some knowledge, they never listened. It was always going in one ear and out the other. That never stopped her though, she still did it anyway, regardless of how bad she got on their nerves. She remembered how it was being their age, with her acting the same way. Yes, she understood all that, but still, she had to do something. She couldn't just sit by and let all of this slide. It would break her heart if either one of them ended up in jail or worse, six feet under.

She replayed everything in her mind. She thought about Toni saying that Mecca and Jeremiah were just like her and Dahlia back in the day, but on steroids. *"WOW!"* she thought, reminiscing on some of the things she had done at their age. Her mind wandered, thinking about the things that her and Dahlia both had done at their age, including all the fighting, and Dahlia eventually going to prison. She thought about the dream that they both had before Dahlia got locked up.

Roro thought about all the things that Mecca and Jeremiah were doing now. *"Hold up!"* she said to herself, remembering the dream that her and Dahlia had some years back about Mecca and Jeremiah. She finally understood it all now. Those dreams weren't made to make her feel crazy, they were simply warnings. This means, that if she's correct... *"Oh Lord, it's happening all over again."*

About The Author

Inspire Wise, a single mother of four, is from Seatack, Virginia, one of the oldest African American communities in the United States, located in Virginia Beach, Virginia. She has firsthand knowledge of life lessons, which caused her to grow wiser with age. She has decided to share that knowledge through her stories, and hopes that everyone can take away something from her words. When she is not writing, she can be found doing hair or passing the time by playing with her lovely grandchildren.

Roro and Dahlia are two best friends raising their sons in Norfolk, Virginia. Dahlia is very humble, and laid back. She always took steps to avoid trouble if she could, however, her sons father Smoke, will go out of his way to make her life a living hell. Her new interest Rodney is the complete opposite. Both are well-known drug dealers and she has to make the decision to play the game or leave it alone.

Roro is straight to the point and the last person you'd want to cross. She's raising the boys to be tough like her, but when she connects with a guy named Jay, it forces her to come face to face with a serious question.. is she setting a good example?

With all of their differences, they both have two things in common, their unconditional love that they mutually share for each other's boys, and their loyalty to their friendship. As their lives both become fueled with chaos and drama, they try to maneuver each obstacle in their way. They do know one thing…they will do whatever is necessary to protect each other…by any means.

Revelation of a Storm by: Inspire Wise